"You know I don't like you, don't you?"

His firm mouth gently teased her delicate lips, taking immediate advantage of their hesitant parting to caress the inner softness with his seeking tongue. His strong fingers lightly stroked the bare skin of her back under her shirt. As his hand moved slowly under her arm and across her ribcage, his lips left the pliant softness of hers to skim lightly down her throat to the rounded tops of her small, firm breasts.

In a harmony of subtle movements his lips pushed aside her blouse and he brought his hand up to cup her breast. "Beautiful," he sighed against her velvety skin. "Just as I said—compact but nice. There's nothing ostentatious about you, princess. Your body is perfectly formed. A goddess in miniature."

Maggie moved her head to kiss the side of his tanned neck. "But you *do* know I don't like you, don't you?" she whispered, breathless from his touch, then tasted his warm skin with the tip of her tongue.

WHAT ARE *LOVESWEPT* ROMANCES?

They are stories of true romance and touching emotion. We believe those two very important ingredients are constants in our highly sensual and very believable stories in the *LOVESWEPT* line. Our goal is to give you, the reader, stories of consistently high quality that may sometimes make you laugh, sometimes make you cry, but are always fresh and creative and contain many delightful surprises within their pages.

Most romance fans read an enormous number of books. Those they truly love, they keep. Others may be traded with friends and soon forgotten. We hope that each *LOVESWEPT* romance will be a treasure—a ''keeper.'' We will always try to publish

LOVE STORIES YOU'LL NEVER FORGET
BY AUTHORS YOU'LL ALWAYS REMEMBER

The Editors

LOVESWEPT · 16

Billie J. Green

A Very Reluctant Knight

BANTAM BOOKS · TORONTO · NEW YORK · LONDON · SYDNEY

A VERY RELUCTANT KNIGHT

A Bantam Book / September 1983

LOVESWEPT and the wave device are trademarks of Bantam Books, Inc.

ISBN 0-553-21616-3

Published simultaneously in the United States and Canada

Bantam Books are published by Bantam Books, Inc. Its trademark, consisting of the words "Bantam Books" and the portrayal of a rooster, is Registered in U.S. Patent and Trademark Office and in other countries. Marca Registrada. Bantam Books, Inc., 666 Fifth Avenue, New York, New York 10103.

PRINTED IN THE UNITED STATES OF AMERICA

O   0 9 8 7 6 5 4 3 2 1

To Nancy—the diminutive dynamo who threatened, cajoled, and frog-marched me into believing in myself.

Chapter One

Maggie will do it.

The familiar words reverberated in her mind, mocking her as she bent to pour the dry dog food into the first of six containers. Sure, she thought in disgust; if no one else wants the job, ask Maggie. She'll do it. Good-hearted, reliable Maggie.

"All right, all right," Maggie muttered in her soft, husky voice as six widely assorted dogs tried noisily to eat from one dish. "I'm going as fast as I can."

The neat, white-fenced yard seemed too small to accommodate the mob of eager dogs. She had never understood how Uncle Charles could have acquired six dogs. Aunt Sarah said he was too soft-hearted to turn away a stray, but then, Aunt Sarah always managed to make everything her husband did sound wonderfully humane, remarkably thoughtful. Maggie couldn't imagine her uncle doing anything that wasn't practical.

1

One simply never knew what motivated others, she thought with a shrug, looking at the proof of his impracticality. She managed to fill four of the containers before being knocked off her feet by an excitable Great Dane. Pulling her five-foot frame upright, she brushed the dirt from her khaki shorts and glared belligerently at the offending animal.

"You want to try that one again, buster?" She took a menacing step forward, and the huge dog licked her hand, humbly begging her pardon with a soft "whoof." "Yes, that's all well and good, but just see that it doesn't happen again."

She struggled among the unruly dogs, pushing them aside to fill the remaining dishes, then looked at the dark clouds building overhead. The sultry, threatening weather suited her mood perfectly. She had been waiting for weeks for Dave to ask her out, and when he finally did, she had been "previously committed"—to babysitting a menagerie of mongrels, for heaven's sake!

Perspiration ran down her chest and was absorbed by the blouse she had tied loosely under her small, rounded breasts, as she pulled a grossly fat dog away from the bowl of a small cocker spaniel. How do I get myself into these situations? she moaned silently. She should have known when Aunt Sarah asked if she had plans for the weekend that it would lead to something like this. It always did.

"I'm a sucker," she told the clamoring dogs. "No." Her gold-tipped brown curls bounced emphatically as she shook her head in a woeful denial of their barked comments. "No, I'm not exaggerating. I tell you, when people see me coming, they don't say, 'Here comes Maggie Simms, the brilliant sales consultant,' or 'Here comes Maggie Simms, the beautiful, vivacious divorcee,' or even 'Here comes Maggie Simms, one heck of a good sport.' No, they say, 'Here comes Maggie Simms—the chump.' "

Framing the friendly Great Dane's head with her small hands, she gazed into his sympathetic brown eyes and said, "Don't you understand? I could have been with Dave this weekend!" She laughed ruefully as a large, wet tongue licked her face consolingly. "Thanks, pal, but I'm afraid it's just not the same."

Minutes later, as the greedy dogs snuffled noisily around in the empty bowls, Maggie leaned against the porch rail of the white frame house, feeling stifled by the heaviness of the air and the futility of her thoughts. She had always enjoyed visiting Aunt Sarah and Uncle Charles in their small East Texas home. The scent of pine in the clean, fresh air was a refreshing change from the heat and exhaust fumes of Dallas. But this weekend was different. If she hadn't promised to watch their beloved brood, she could have been with the only man she had found interesting since her divorce.

Dave was the new man at the office. The company had transferred him from Houston to replace Maggie's retiring supervisor. Dave's shy smile and slender, but good looking frame had attracted her immediately. She had watched as he had put her coworkers at ease, demonstrating his authority with thoughtfulness and diplomacy, avoiding office politics. His quiet intelligence had a way of calming even the most troubled waters, and he had already gained the respect of his superiors.

Recently divorced, he was the target of a lot of

lively speculation and gossip, but so far he had not paid noticeable attention to any of the attractive women in the building. Several times, however, Maggie had turned to find him watching her with a gleam of interest in his pale blue eyes.

Then, on Thursday, in the middle of a casual conversation, he had asked her to attend a concert with him. She had had to force a refusal from her lips. After all the overconfident males Maggie had met since her divorce, Dave's shyness was like a breath of fresh air. And, best of all, he was only seven inches taller than she. Her neck had a permanent crick from looking up at her previous dates.

Maggie sighed in regret and looked around her at the beautiful country setting. If there were any justice at all, she would be preparing for her date with Dave instead of watching a storm build.

The dark clouds now hung low over the open fields behind the house, convincing her that it was time to start securing the windows. She pushed away from the rail just as a large silver Mercedes passed the house, throwing up a choking cloud of dust from the dirt road.

"Thanks," she muttered darkly. "That's all I need. Add that to all my perspiration and it makes a real nice layer of mud." She glared impotently after the disappearing vehicle, then stared in surprise as it pulled to a stop and began to back up. When it reached the front gate set in the white picket fence, it stopped. The man inside turned off the ignition and got out of the car.

Speaking of king-sized—the man was Brobdingnagian, one of those giants straight out of *Gulliver's Travels.* Several inches over six feet, he moved with the agile grace of a sleek greyhound.

His handsome, lightly tanned face held a casual, almost bored expression, but there was nothing dilatory in his movements. Even from a distance Maggie recognized the dynamic energy vibrating from his lean, hard body. His superbly cut suit, which he wore with the careless ease of one used to such things, looked out of place in this homey setting, his dark-blond hair and refined features giving him the aristocratic look of Scandinavian nobility.

A Norse god in the flesh, she thought impudently as he swung open the gate and walked toward her. "Hello." She smiled her welcome with the courtesy that was a deeply ingrained part of her nature. Although she very much resented the way he eyed her bare midriff and shapely tanned legs, she kept the polite smile glued firmly in place. "Is there something I can do for you?"

"I certainly hope so," he said silkily.

His voice was deep and refined, and a practiced smile played about his perfectly sculptured lips. His steady examination of her face made her tingle in discomfort as she waited for him to continue.

"I thought perhaps you could tell me if this road will take me to the Kingman Lodge," he asked smoothly.

Is that the best you can do? she scoffed silently. There were signs every five hundred feet that led straight to the lodge, which was located on a small, privately owned lake several miles west of her uncle's home—a fact that this Lothario knew full well. And what was more, judging by the amused gleam in his unusual silver-gray eyes, he knew she was aware of his knowledge. Wonderful, she mused sarcastically. With all my problems, I have to run across a full-fledged nut with a kinky yen for sweaty, dust-covered country bumpkins.

Refusing to comment on the transparency of his gambit, she sighed deeply, then answered politely. "Yes, it will."

He looked at her face for a long moment, then dropped his gaze to her breasts. Maggie caught her breath sharply at the caressing quality of his look. Here it comes, she thought, mentally preparing to parry his advances.

"Thank you," he said quietly; then, incredibly, turned to walk back toward the gate.

The oversized idiot was leaving! He had actually stopped to confirm his directions, she thought in amazement, watching his lithe figure as he strode across the yard and out the gate.

On the other side of the Mercedes he halted, looking at her across the silver top with an amused twinkle in his strange eyes. "By the way," he remarked casually, "while you were rolling around in the dirt, your shirt came unbuttoned." His smile broadened audaciously as he heard her gasp and saw her hand fly up to cover her partially exposed breasts. "Very nice. Compact, but nice," he added in a soft murmur, then opened the door and folded his tall frame into the driver's seat.

"Insufferable man," she muttered as the car disappeared in a cloud of dust. He could at least have refrained from mentioning it. Turning abruptly, she walked indignantly into the house.

Two hours later, a shower and clean clothing had restored her, mentally as well as physically. As she rocked gently in the porch swing, she decided with a good-humored grin that she had deserved that man's parting shot. She had begun making ridiculous assumptions about him the minute he stepped from his car. While she still thought his reason for stopping was highly suspect, there had been no excuse for prejudging him.

Maggie looked into the gathering darkness and admitted that mentally she had been punishing the man simply because he wasn't Dave. Dave would never in a million years have had that superior, knowing look in his eyes. He was gentle and sensible and honorable. And after her disastrous six years with Barry, she appreciated those three qualities as she never had before.

Barry had seemed like a charming child. Tall and beautifully formed, he had taken what the world—including Maggie—had handed him as though it were his due.

Born to middle-class parents, Barry had been outrageously spoiled by his mother. She had deprived her other children of luxuries so that her last-born could have whatever took his fancy, and Barry had come to expect that kind of sacrifice.

Stunned by his physical beauty and charming, boyish facade, Maggie had taken over from Barry's mother, willing, even eager to do whatever she could to make him happy. She soon found that money was necessary to keep Barry in the manner to which he had become accustomed, so she had worked long hours babying their small printing business along until it was at last a financial success. Perhaps she had worked too hard. Somewhere along the line the urge to please Barry—which had proven an impossible task anyway—had been superceded by a personal need for success. And a wife who was absent for most of the time and dead tired when she was home couldn't have been very pleasant. But Maggie had been the practical one in their marriage. A doer tied to a dreamer. Slowly she had come to realize that Barry resented the very thing that had drawn him to her in the beginning—her strength and her drive.

She stood in agitation as the thoughts she had carefully kept buried for two years crept into her mind. Henry, her Great Dane friend, joined her on the porch nuzzling her hand in a vain attempt to comfort.

If only I could have given more of the responsibility to Barry, she thought. If Maggie had been weaker, perhaps he would have been stronger. But she had seen early in their marriage that Barry was simply not capable of handling responsibility. Every time she had encouraged him to take part in the operation of their budding business, he had botched the simplest tasks.

As she paced back and forth across the porch, her slender figure tense, the huge black dog matched her steps, looking up occasionally with sympathetic eyes.

"I tried, Henry," she told the friendly beast, her soft, husky voice sounding vaguely regretful. "I tried to be what he wanted, but I simply can't be weak and brainless."

When Barry had finally admitted he had been having an affair for over six months, Maggie had felt like an utter fool. It had never occurred to her that he would be unfaithful. An oddity in this supposedly enlightened age of disposable relationships, she'd believed that marriage was forever. "Till death do us part," she thought cynically . . . or at least until he didn't need me any more.

But as faulty as their marriage had been, Maggie had fought tooth and nail for its survival—until she realized that Barry's new love had a weapon that beat anything in Maggie's arsenal. Barry felt sorry for the woman.

She had more problems than any ten women I know, Maggie sighed mournfully. And on top of all her physical and financial woes, her apartment was overrun with bugs. During the many arguments that marked the end of their marriage, Barry had always returned to that fact as an example of how much his intended needed him.

"Lord, Henry." Maggie stopped pacing and looked into the soulful brown eyes that watched her closely. "If I had known he wanted bugs, I would have had them shipped in!"

But she couldn't pretend to be other than she really was, so she had given in, and she counted the divorce a personal failure. She knew she had either failed in her choice of a life partner or she had failed as a woman. Either one was a devastating blow to her self-esteem.

Weakened emotionally by doubt and self-blame, she had not fought Barry's claim to their printing business. So at the age of twenty-nine she had found herself without a husband and without the business for which she had worked so hard. Although she didn't regret breaking her ties with the past by turning over the shop to Barry and his new wife, seeing it die slowly through mismanagement had broken her heart, and she had learned to avoid the small side street where it was located.

Her job as sales consultant with Howard Electronics had been a lifesaver. Throwing herself into her job, she had adapted quickly to her new life style, and the friends she had made at work kept her too busy for idle speculation about the past.

Now, two years later, she had at last met a man

she felt she could trust. Dave had none of Barry's showy male beauty. He was attractive in a quiet, understated way. He was thoughtful and interested in the people around him, whereas Barry had been interested only in what benefited Barry.

Maggie shook free of her depressing thoughts of the past and looked again into the darkening afternoon around her, this time with a hint of bewilderment. It was only four o'clock. It shouldn't be this dark for another three hours. The air had an eerie blue cast, and there was not a breath of wind, the strange stillness somehow menacing.

As she stood and walked into the yard to survey the surrounding dark clouds, she heard a car approaching. The silver gleam was recognizable even in the blue-tinted shadows. The arrogant stranger had obviously finished whatever business had taken him to the isolated lodge. The lodge and lake were frequently rented for company parties or for tired executives to enjoy a weekend of quiet, undisturbed fishing. But somehow Maggie couldn't visualize that particular man doing anything as mundane as arranging a rental. His car slowed to a crawl as it passed the house, and she resisted a childish urge to poke out her tongue as she saw his head turn to take in her jean-clad—and, thankfully, clean—form. Suddenly the car screeched to a halt and he was hurtling through the gate to grab her roughly by the shoulders.

"What in the hell are you doing?" she squeaked, slapping ineffectually at the hands that were digging painfully into her skin.

"Look!" he commanded urgently, turning her body to face the fields behind the house.

The low clouds were rolling and swirling furiously. And three fields away a slender, snaking tail hung down from the angry mass, taking terrifying shape before her eyes.

"My God," she breathed in awe. "A tornado. It's spectacular." Her whispered words were barely audible. "Grim, but somehow magnificent and elemental."

"Look, love," he said drily, "unless you want to get your camera and take pictures, I think it's time we made our move."

"The cellar!" she exclaimed, pulling her eyes away from the mesmerizing force of the gray funnel.

She grabbed his hand and began to run. Behind the house, Maggie headed for a mound of grass-covered earth. As he swung the metal door wide on its hinges and began to push her inside, she recalled the reason for her stay. "The dogs! I've got to get the dogs!"

"There's no time," he shouted impatiently, shoving her into the cellar before him, then pulling the heavy door shut with a loud thud.

The sound of her own breathing seemed unnaturally loud in the sudden silence as Maggie moved cautiously down the wooden steps. At the bottom she stood stock still, paralyzed by the engulfing darkness around her, the musty smell of damp earth invading her nostrils. "There's a light pull somewhere," she said nervously, shuddering at the thought of the snakes that continually sought refuge in the cellar.

She stumbled forward with a startled squeak as the tall figure behind her bumped into her, then caught her breath in a gasp of pure terror as something soft and slithery brushed her face. Breathing an audible sigh of relief, she realized it was the string of the elusive light pull and grasped it firmly, turning on the dim bulb in the ceiling of the small room.

Maggie hadn't been in the cellar since she was a child, and as she looked around, a variety of childhood memories came flooding back. Memories of long, lazy summers. Of playing tag with her cousin Chuck. Of helping Aunt Sarah can fruit and vegetables in a steaming hot kitchen, then storing the labeled jars on the shelves of this wonderfully cool place.

"We might as well be comfortable while we await the tempest," the man said in a lazy, amused voice.

Maggie had completely forgotten the stranger. He had moved a stack of burlap bags from a wide bench to the floor and was removing his jacket, hanging it neatly on a peg on the wall. He must have taken off his tie earlier, for his white shirt was opened wide at the neck.

"How long do you think it will be?" she asked, joining him hesitantly on the bench. "It looked awfully close."

"Most tornadoes move about ten miles per hour, I believe." His voice sounded casual, almost uninterested. "I should say the whole thing will be over in a few minutes."

"I wish I could have gotten the dogs. Uncle Charles will kill me if anything happens to them," she said anxiously.

He leaned comfortably against the wall, stretching out his long legs, and looked around the cellar. "The dogs will be fine."

Maggie shifted uneasily when he stopped his examination of the room to look her up and down as though she were a slave he was thinking seriously about purchasing, his curious gray eyes glinting in amusement at her discomfort.

"Dogs have the uncanny ability of sensing natural danger," he continued, sounding unutterably bored with the subject. "They'll take cover until all danger has passed. Besides, I can't really see us cooped up in this tiny place with all those dogs. It would be total chaos."

And they might rumple your suit, she thought sarcastically. You pompous ass! I'd rather have the dogs for company.

Suddenly the quiet was broken by a thundering crash that shook the cement floor beneath them. The Furies had pursued them into the underworld. Maggie shrieked in terror as their dim light was extinguished and jars leaped from the shelves to shatter on the floor all around them. She felt herself being jerked abruptly from her cowering position on the bench; then she was lying on the floor under the bench, held in a fierce grip by the man who now represented security in their underground world gone mad.

She shook in fright for what seemed like hours, hugging him tightly around the waist as he held her wedged between his body and the wall. Quiet reined for some time before she was calm enough to loosen her hold and whisper softly, "Do you think it's over now?"

His face was buried in her short brown curls, and she felt his husky whisper on her sensitive scalp. "You've never been in a tornado before?"

"No, thank God," came her heartfelt reply.

"There is sometimes a lull like this before the worst part." He sounded serious and concerned—almost too much so—and there was a strange undertone of something—amusement, perhaps?

—in his deep voice. "Just to make sure, we had better stay where we are for a while." He pulled her closer, shaping her tiny frame to his long, hard body.

"How . . ." Her voice was a thin imitation of its natural soft huskiness. She cleared her throat to begin again. "How long?"

"That's difficult to say." His mouth had moved closer, a hair's-breadth away from her tingling ear. "It could be as much as an hour. But believe me, I'll know when it's time to leave." His long-fingered hand moved to rest just below one small breast. "Don't you think it's time we introduced ourselves? My name is Mark Wilding."

"How do you do? I'm . . . I'm . . . What are you doing with your hand?" she gasped as his hand moved a fraction of an inch higher.

"Just checking your body temperature and pulse, love," he explained smoothly. That curious undertone in his voice was stronger now. "I want to be sure you're not in shock."

"I'm perfectly fine, thank you, so you can move your hand," she said stiffly. "And my name is Maggie Simms."

"Maggie. Is that a diminutive of Margaret?" he asked politely as his hand moved over the smooth line of her trim hip.

Maggie shivered in unbidden pleasure as she felt the warmth of his palm through the denim of her jeans. Steeling herself against his insidious touch, she pulled his hand to her waist. "No, it's just plain Maggie," she stated firmly, determined to win the battle of wills.

He moved one hard thigh until it rested on hers, slipping his hand around to stroke her back beneath her loose cotton top. "Were you named for your mother?" he whispered, his lips moving against her ear.

Her small hand dug into his thigh as she shoved it away, then with her elbow she pushed down on his arm until it rested again on her waist. "No, my parents simply liked the name," she said through clenched teeth.

But the roving hand didn't stop for long at her waist. After a barely perceptible pause, it continued down to mold one firm buttock, and his knee moved suggestively against her leg. "I believe one of my maternal great-aunts was named Maggie," he murmured huskily.

Reaching behind her back, she dug her nails into the strong hand and forcibly shoved it back around to his chest, her tennis shoe connecting with his shin at the same moment. "It's very possible. The name is not uncommon," she panted, out of breath.

An imperceptible movement brought the back of his hand against her breast, where it gently brushed one sensitive nipple through the soft fabric. "It's a very pleasant-sounding name, with practical, even earthy, connotations." He took the lobe of her ear between his teeth in a soft, erotic nip.

"It serves its purpose," she gasped, tilting her head to avoid his persistent lips, then pulling his hand away from the hardening tip of her breast to hold it firmly between both of hers.

"Yes, I'm sure it does." His lips moved to her exposed neck as though she had offered it purposely for his pleasure. He brought her hands to his chest, pushing one inside the open neck of his shirt.

The sensual feel of his warm, hair-roughened

chest beneath her small hand was the last straw, and Maggie groaned in defeat, bringing her free hand up to grasp his neck as he sought her sensitive lips with his own. In a swift sideways movement he half-covered her soft body with his lean, hard frame.

His firm mouth gently teased her delicate lips, taking immediate advantage of their hesitant parting to caress the inner softness with his seeking tongue. His strong fingers lightly stroked the bare skin of her back under her shirt. As his hand moved slowly under her arm and across her rib cage, his lips left the pliant softness of hers to skim lightly down her throat to the rounded tops of her small, firm breasts.

In a harmony of subtle movements his lips pushed aside her blouse, and he brought his hand up to cup her breast. "Beautiful," he sighed against her velvety skin. "Just as I said—compact, but nice. There's nothing ostentatious about you, princess. Your body is perfectly formed. A goddess in miniature."

Maggie moved her head to kiss the side of his tanned neck. "You know I don't like you, don't you?" she whispered, breathless from his touch, then tasted his warm skin with the tip of her tongue.

He groaned at the sensual caress and murmured huskily, "Yes, I know, love," then found the taut tip of her breast with his stroking thumb. "God, I love that husky little voice of yours."

He moved his head to reclaim her lips, and Maggie went under for the third time. She brought her hands to his neck, smoothing the taut sinews. His bold tongue caressed the moist sweetness of hers, discovering and memorizing the depths of pleasure to shake her slender body.

"As soon as we're able to leave," he murmured against her tender lips, "shall we continue this charming enterprise in more comfortable surroundings?"

The softly spoken words filtered temptingly into her brain, then brought her to the surface with a shuddering jolt. She was letting the arrogant fool make love to her! "No!" she gasped, her voice weak. She pulled away as far as the wall behind her would permit.

"I told you before, Mr. Wilding, I don't like you." Her voice was firmer now. Her eyes had adjusted to the dark, and she looked at his face as she spoke. "And I don't like the idea of your taking advantage of the situation to try to amuse yourself." She straightened her blouse with a jerk. "Just because my body is small doesn't mean my brain is undersized as well. I may have gotten a little carried away—it's been a very tense evening—but don't think I'm stupid enough to play along with a supercilious playboy who's out for a roll in the hay with a local peasant just to pass the time!"

"You're absolutely adorable!" He chuckled in delight, reaching out to pull her close again.

"But you've got a tile loose," she muttered under her breath, pushing against the solid wall of his chest.

"You look like a little Bantam hen with its feathers all ruffled," he laughed, trying to still her struggling body.

"Huh!" she snorted inelegantly. "Bantam hen, my foot. I'll bet my Aunt Martha's teeth you've never even seen a Banty."

"You know," he said in surprise, "I believe you're

right. I haven't. That just shows you should feel sorry for me. I had a deprived childhood."

"I'm sure the only things you were deprived of were spankings," she said maliciously. "Now, let me go, you insensitive clod!" She shoved her small fist into his stomach with as much force as her confined circumstances allowed.

"But, love," he objected, wheezing slightly from the blow, "can't we discuss this?" Suddenly he jerked upright, banging his head on the bench as a blood-curdling howl filtered through the door and echoed eerily around their miniature cavern.

"My Lord!" he exclaimed, rubbing the top of his injured head. "The keening of the hounds of the Baskervilles, no doubt."

"Henry!" Maggie said, recognizing the howl of her sympathetic friend. She scrambled over Mark's prone figure and stood upright. "That must mean it's safe to go out."

"Watch the broken glass, for heaven's sake," he warned irritably. "Those flimsy sneakers you're wearing aren't much protection. Just stay where you are. I'll go open the door and show the miserable beast that you're still alive."

Maggie stifled a snicker at his disgruntled tone, relieved to be rescued from what was turning out to be a very awkward situation. She waited patiently at the foot of the stairs, listening with a satisfied smile to the duet of his grumbling, unintelligible comments and the piercing howls of the Great Dane. She heard a muffled thud as Mark shoved against the door with his shoulder. Seconds later he swore viciously and she heard louder, more forceful thuds.

"What's wrong?" she asked anxiously as the unmistakable sound of his descending footsteps reached her ears. When he was standing before her she could see surprise etched on his handsome features.

He rubbed his jaw thoughtfully. "I'm sorry, Maggie, but it appears we'll be here for a while. His voice was guarded, and he watched her closely as he continued. "The door seems to be blocked from the outside."

Chapter Two

"Blocked? What do you mean, blocked?" she asked, confused. "How can it be blocked?"

"By blocked I mean obstructed or barricaded," he explained with irritating patience, a grin of genuine amusement taking the place of his practiced smile. He placed his foot on the bench beside her, resting his forearm leisurely on his knee, and looked her up and down, a speculative gleam showing in his clear gray eyes. "And as to how it came to be blocked, I'd put my money on the tree that was growing several yards from the cellar door."

"Aunt Sarah's magnolia tree!" she gasped in horror. "But she loved that tree. She planted it the year she and Uncle Charles were married."

"Although your aunt has my deepest sympathy," he said, "I'm afraid the demise of her tree is the least of our worries right now. Apparently it's fallen across the door, and"—he paused dramatically, then dropped his voice to a whisper, watching her face as he spoke to see if his words were sinking in—"we are trapped . . . together . . . alone . . . in a very small, very dark cellar. *Capisci?*"

"Oh, no," she moaned, eyeing him warily, at last grasping the full import of his words. She backed slowly away from him and his smug, knowing grin.

"Oh, yes, love. It should be interesting, to say the least." He chuckled in satisfaction. "Now, where were we before we were so rudely interrupted?"

"Hen-ry!" she screeched, her voice rising on the last syllable. Then, turning sharply, Maggie raced through the broken glass and up the stairs as surefooted as though each step were planned in advance instead of being the result of blind panic. She pressed urgently against the door with her shoulder. When it refused to budge, she kicked it viciously, yelping—more in annoyance than in pain—when she bruised her foot. Then, in a frustrated fit of pique, she beat against the metal door with her fists, all to the accompaniment of Henry's excited barks.

At last, realizing she was accomplishing nothing except perhaps to make herself look foolish, she leaned her head against the door and took deep, steadying breaths. The sound of crunching glass brought her head up sharply, and she peered over her shoulder into the darkness below. She could barely make out his tall shape at the foot of the stairs as his disgruntled reprimand floated softly up to her ears.

"All that energy wasted on a *door.*"

Oh, Lord, she moaned silently. She was trapped underground with an overbred, oversexed octopus, and there was nothing she could do about it. At least, she thought, squaring her shoulders, there is nothing I can do about escaping, but I'll be damned if I'll let that arrogant behemoth chase me around the cellar until my aunt and uncle return on Sunday.

Standing straight, and as tall as one can when one is five feet nothing, she marched down the stairs, moving Mark abruptly to one side, and said briskly, "There was always a kerosene lamp on one of these shelves. I'm sure my aunt and uncle haven't changed their habits and keep the lamp primed for an emergency like this. But the first thing to do is clean up this mess so that we can move without stepping on glass." If it did come down to playing tag, Maggie at least wanted a clear running field. "If you'll look to your immediate right you should find it along with the matches."

She held her breath, waiting for his reaction, then gave a sigh of relief as she heard him strike a match and saw the lamp in the faint glow. Thank heaven it hadn't been destroyed in the turbulence earlier.

Mark lit the lamp and placed it on a shelf beside the bench, whistling cheerfully as he moved, then turned to face her in the dim light, saluting smartly. "What now, Captain?" he asked briskly, grinning devilishly at her obvious irritation.

"Oh, for heaven's sake," she muttered, "just sit on the bench and stay out of my way until I finish."

"But I wouldn't dream of letting you do all the work," he argued. "Hand me the broom and I'll have it clear in no time at all."

"I doubt very seriously you would know what to

do with a broom. And besides," she added maliciously, "you might get your hands dirty."

"No!" he exclaimed in mock horror. "In that case perhaps you had better do it yourself. Judging from the first time I saw you, you're particularly fond of dirt, and I wouldn't want to deprive you of the pleasure."

As Maggie sputtered indignantly, he turned and walked to the bench. After clearing it of a few fragments of glass, he sat down, his arms folded, then leaned back against the wall, watching her closely, a waiting look in his gray eyes.

Clearing her throat nervously, she turned her back on his disconcerting stare, lifted the push broom from the corner, and began to shove vigorously at the broken glass, thankful that most of the filled jars had stayed on the shelves. As she worked she glanced frequently over her shoulder at him, waiting for she knew not what. Each time he would merely smile inquiringly, occasionally stifling a bored yawn, but never once taking his eyes from her.

When she had done all she could, she slowly replaced the broom, then stood facing the wall, feeling a perfect imbecile. Now what? she thought desperately. If he had shown signs of aggression she could have handled it, but his silent waiting was driving her crazy.

Careful, Maggie, she told herself, you're letting him get to you. She turned abruptly to face him. He was leaning against the wall, still watching, still waiting. As she stared he moved his arm to pat the bench beside him, suppressed laughter sparkling in his eyes.

The elegant jackass is teasing me! she thought, feeling momentary relief. Then fury began to seep

into her veins. As if being trapped weren't bad
enough! No, she had to be trapped with a damned
comedian. She glared at him coldly, but the only
effect was a broadening of his smile.

"Come and sit down, Maggie," he said softly.
"You must be tired after all that work."

"No, thank you," she replied icily. "I'd rather
stand."

"For two days?" he queried in disbelief. "Your
aunt and uncle aren't due back until Sunday
evening, so we might as well resign ourselves to a
long wait."

Astonishment froze her features. "How did you
know?" she whispered, staring at his handsome
face as if he were the devil himself.

"Jake told me," he replied, as though it were
obvious.

"Jake? Jake? Why should he tell you about
my aunt and uncle?" she asked in confusion.
Jake owned the Kingman Lodge and was Uncle
Charles's best friend. Maggie had known him all
her life, and she would have bet anything that he
was not the kind of man who discussed other
people's business with strangers.

"Because I asked," he said simply. "And perhaps because I'm his favorite nephew."

"Jake is your uncle? I don't believe it," she stated
flatly. "That sweet old man couldn't possibly have
a nephew like you."

"He does, I assure you." Her astonishment
seemed to add to his amusement.

"Then why has he never mentioned you?" she
asked suspiciously.

Mark rose to his feet, casually stretching his
lean frame, and walked toward her as he spoke.
"Would you call Jake a garrulous man?"

Backing up a step, she eyed his advancing form warily. "No, I would not. Which makes it even stranger that he should suddenly become so talkative with you." Her words came out as an unequivocal accusation.

"That was different—I asked," he said reasonably, still walking casually in her direction. "I'm sure if you had asked, he would have been glad to tell you all about his attractive, talented nephew."

"And just exactly what made you ask about my aunt and uncle?" Her cautious retreat was halted abruptly as she backed into the shelves lining the wall.

"Actually, I didn't mention either of those worthy people." He was only steps away now, giving every appearance of enjoying himself immensely. "I asked about a beautiful but haughty featherweight with gold-tipped brown hair and gold-flecked brown eyes." There was a subtle difference in his voice, and the softly murmured words were like invisible caresses that lingered in the air and on her sensitive skin long after he finished speaking. Staring intently at the fluttering movement of her small breasts as the rate of her breathing increased sharply, he added in a husky whisper, "I knew what it would be like to hold you the moment I saw you. But I underestimated the feeling. It was incredibly right, Maggie."

Mesmerized, her eyes followed his slow movement forward as a cobra follows the movement of a snake charmer's flute. He was a step away, lifting his arms to enfold her, when she shook free of his spell. Searching frantically for something stronger than her will to hold him off, she found only the jars on the shelves that were pressing uncomfortably into her back. Grasping the largest jar she saw, she held it threateningly high.

"Stay back," she warned. "Take one more step and I'll hit you with this jar of"—she glanced at the jar—"chow-chow."

He stood abruptly still, shock spreading across his perfect face. Then, incredibly, he began to laugh. His laughter grew, echoing richly in the small room, until he was holding his sides weakly. Just as he was beginning to control it, he glanced at Maggie's features, and the perplexed astonishment in her features set him off once again.

"Foiled by a jar of chow-chow," he gasped, finally settling down to a chuckle. "Maggie, you're wonderful! But tell me, sweetheart, what exactly is chow-chow?"

His laughter was so natural, so irresistible, she found herself grinning too. "It's a relish made of . . ." Maggie paused as he moved oh, so casually closer to her, ostensibly to examine the jar. "It doesn't really matter, does it? What does matter, Mr. Wilding, is the fact that I don't want you to make love to me. So would you please cut out the playboy stuff? It's very wearing on the nerves." As she spoke she realized she was addressing him as an equal for the first time and felt vaguely ashamed of herself.

"Of course," he replied matter-of-factly. "I wouldn't dream of pushing in where I'm not wanted." His innocent expression was just a shade overdone. "But tell me, *Ms. Simms*, just exactly what is it about me that you don't like?"

His curiosity seemed genuine, causing Maggie to search for solid reasons to explain her dislike. However, nothing that came to mind seemed an adequate explanation for the instant antagonism she had felt. Feeling defensive, which was probably what he had intended all along, she blurted out, "You're too tall."

"So I'll slump," he said agreeably, making his actions suit his words. "Anything else?"

"Is this necessary? Can't we just put it down to chemistry?" The wicked gleam that appeared in his eyes at the last word reminded her of the sensual sparks that had flown between them earlier. She cleared her throat nervously. "Oh, very well. I've never cared for fair men, and your attitude toward life is the antithesis of mine."

"You're very sharp," he observed lazily, "to have interpreted my attitude toward life in the space of"—he glanced at his watch—"two hours and fifteen minutes." He paused and watched her shift uncomfortably. "What you're trying to say is that I remind you of your ex-husband, right?"

"How did you? . . . Of course. Jake told you about Barry, too." She moved past him in annoyance. "Jake talks too damn much."

He watched her irritated pacing for a moment. "I'm sorry, Maggie. Forget I said that. Come sit down and relax." When she threw him a doubtful look over her shoulder, he added, "We'll simply talk—I swear."

Maggie shrugged wearily, tired of running and tired of the way the past kept popping up this evening. That was all behind her, and she wanted to forget it. She sat on the bench, glancing at him warily but not protesting when he settled her comfortably against his shoulder.

"You poor baby. You're all worn out, aren't you?" he asked softly. "I'm sorry I gave you such a hard time. I suppose I acted from habit. Although that's not an adequate excuse, it's the only one I have—

unless you count a stupendous craving for your body."

"Do you realize what you're saying?" she murmured sleepily, pointedly ignoring his last comment. "You've just admitted that you normally view women as sex objects. Didn't you know that the male chauvinist is on his way out?" She chuckled lazily. "If you're not careful, you'll find yourself in the same fix as the dinosaur."

"I'm sorry to disillusion you, love," he murmured drily, "but there are some women who can be viewed in no other way. Perhaps it's different in your world, but so many of the people I meet— male and female—are only too eager to trade their integrity for filthy lucre—or its equivalent."

The amused cynicism in his voice brought her eyes to his face in curiosity. But there was something besides cynicism in his silver eyes. Something that Maggie didn't want to recognize, for it made him too human. A sadness, perhaps even loneliness, that didn't show in his lazily drawled words. She buried the thought quickly, saying in a casual voice, "I suppose everyone has wondered at one time or another what it would be like to be one of the beautiful people, but to tell you the truth, I never felt I would enjoy that kind of life. It seems to me that it would be the most boring thing in the world. If you could have anything you wanted, you would have to search continually for a new and different high. It seems that it would breed a terrible kind of desperation."

Mark looked at her thoughtfully for a moment with something resembling respect in his eyes. "Amazing," he murmured, then smiled wryly. "You're right, of course. Not that it's that way for everyone. Some are lucky enough to find something solid to anchor them—their work or, more rarely, a special person to love. But too often the person who has everything has nothing."

Just as she was—reluctantly—beginning to be moved by what he seemed to be admitting, his face was transformed by a mischievous grin, and he said, "Didn't I tell you that you should pity me?"

"You're incorrigible," she said, exasperated. "I think I would be wasting my time feeling sorry for you. I also think that wealth is wasted on the wealthy. If I had money I think I'd be a full-time student. There's so much to learn," she explained thoughtfully. "Or maybe I would be a part-time student and spend the rest of the time seeing the world."

"Have you done much traveling?" he asked, smiling, his mood of moments before seeming a figment of her imagination.

"If you count trips to Oklahoma to see Aunt Martha, I guess the answer would still be no," she laughingly admitted.

"But you would like to?"

"Who wouldn't?" she asked, puzzled by the strange light appearing in his eyes.

"How would you like to go to St. Thomas?" At her baffled look, he continued. "I have to fly to Charlotte Amalie next weekend on business. Come with me."

"Mark," she reproved. "I thought you were going to behave!"

"Maggie, you'll love the Virgin Islands," he said, ignoring her reprimand. "Even though they're over-run with tourists, they're still the most charming islands you could imagine. My business wouldn't take long, and we would have plenty of time to explore. How about it?" he coaxed.

"Mark, you're impossible! You were just speaking of people who trade their integrity for the things money can buy. Now you're trying to make me one of them." She looked at him sternly. "Unless you want me to believe that you mean for the trip to be strictly platonic."

He chuckled. "I may be a little warped, love, but I'm not masochistic. I can't imagine you and me having a platonic relationship."

"And I can't imagine our having any kind of relationship at all," she stated firmly. "Once we're out of here, we'll never see each other again. We don't move in the same circles. You're name brand and I'm generic, and never the twain shall meet. *Capisci*?" Her tone mimicked his polished accent.

"Maggie, Maggie." He laughed. "I may be name brand, but I defy anyone to label you. You, love, are strictly one of a kind. Which is why I don't intend to let you disappear out of my life." He hugged her briefly, then said, "Tell me about your ex-husband. I get the feeling I'm taking some of his blows, so perhaps I had better know more about him."

"There's not really much to tell." She sighed, wondering wryly why the past would not die gracefully instead of popping up when she least expected it. "Barry was charming and extremely good-looking. He was also greedy and self-centered. I think it's something that he had no control over. In any situation that arose, his first thought was how it would affect him. He simply wasn't able to consider anyone else's feelings." She paused, thoughtfully considering her next remarks. "There was something lacking in his character, and that lack stunted his emotional growth. It was sad, actually. He missed so much by constantly looking inward." Sighing regretfully, she continued. "At first I hoped Elise, his current wife, would bring out some latent caring in Barry, but now I doubt it. He's caring when it suits his purpose or when it's convenient." Suddenly finding herself feeling the frustration of those years, she asked, "Why are we talking about this? It's not my idea of a pleasant topic."

"I thought perhaps if I understood your relationship with Barry, I might find the chink in your armor." He gave her an exaggerated leer. "Which would make it easier to seduce you."

Maggie chuckled, not feeling threatened by his teasing. "I have no chinks in my armor, and now that you mention it, I had no relationship with Barry. I thought I did at the time, but it was all in my mind." She smiled in reminiscence. "Dr. Ames forced me to admit that I had fought the divorce not because I wanted Barry, but because I didn't want to admit my marriage was a failure. He finally convinced me that even I—Maggie Perfect— am allowed to fail occasionally."

"He sounds like a wise man. Who is he?"

"He's the psychiatrist at the clinic that I entered after . . ." She grinned impishly as she remembered the events that led up to her stay at the clinic.

"After what?" he asked, his curiosity aroused.

"When Barry didn't come home one night, I called Elise, and of course, he was there. I told him I had changed my mind. He could have the divorce and our printing business. Then I took all his beautiful, expensive suits that I broke my back to buy, put them into the bathtub, and doused them with his lovely—and also expensive—cognac."

"And then?" he asked, grinning widely as he anticipated her next words.

"Then I threw in a lighted match and *then* I admitted myself to the mental clinic."

"Why, for heaven's sake?"

"I had never lost my temper to that extent," she explained. "I didn't consider my actions rational. It took Dr. Ames two weeks to convince me that I had handled my anger in a way that was harmful to no one. He said if I had doused *Barry* with the cognac and set him alight, then he might consider treating me, but under the circumstances, he needed the bed space."

"I was right," Mark murmured softly. "You are one of a kind. As tough as an army sergeant and as vulnerable as a baby sparrow."

"No, not vulnerable," she denied, shaking her head, her gold-tipped curls catching the soft lamplight. "Not any more."

"You think not?" he whispered, smiling as though she had issued a challenge. "Come with me to St. Thomas and we'll see who's right." His hand cradling her shoulder suddenly became electrified, causing the skin beneath it to tingle in the most peculiar way. A gentle movement of his long fingers spread the sensation across her upper body, and she shivered in a dangerously sensual response.

"Mark," she whispered huskily. Her voice held a vaguely pleading note, and for a moment she wasn't sure whether she was pleading for him to stop or to continue. "Mark," she said, her voice firmer, "I've already told you that I won't go with you. Can we please drop the subject? And I thought we had decided earlier that there would be no more hanky-panky."

"Hanky-panky?" He chuckled. "Where on earth do you pick up words like that? And for the record, love, you decided. I was coerced into agreeing." He laughed softly. "Perhaps I'd better warn you that I've been known to lie to get what I want."

"You're admitting that you would stoop to a lie just to get your own way?" she asked in astonished disbelief.

"Admirably honest of me, don't you think?" he asked with an audacious smile of satisfaction.

Maggie drew back and looked at his complacent features. "I think, Mr. Mark Wilding," she said with grudging admiration, "that you are totally untrustworthy, and I wouldn't be surprised if you were lying about lying."

"Oh, no. I'm absolutely serious," he vowed. "My one character defect is not handling defeat well—so I simply avoid it, then at the very least I retain the appearance of perfection."

"All that and humility, too," she said and laughed.

"Of course. Now you're getting a glimmer of what you're passing up by not going with me."

"I'm sure I'll hate myself for not jumping at the chance," she said, beginning to enjoy his offbeat sense of humor. "But I guess I'm just too dim-witted to recognize the opportunity of a lifetime."

He patted her consolingly on the shoulder. "Don't worry about it, love. I have occasionally run across someone who doesn't appreciate my true worth, but I eventually manage to convince even the most stubborn skeptic."

"I'll just bet you do," she muttered, stifling a sleepy yawn. "And it appears you'll have plenty of time to convert me." She looked around the cellar. "Two days, in fact. Mark, what are we going to do about a place to sleep? This floor is concrete."

"Don't worry, princess. While you were playing janitor I was scouting the territory . . ." He intercepted her indignant glance, as she recalled the way he had watched her so intently, and added quickly, with injured innocence, ". . . for sleeping accommodations."

"Uh-huh," she agreed skeptically. "And what did you find?"

He stood and moved to where he had stacked the burlap bags earlier. "The burlap will do for a mattress." He picked up a canvas tarpaulin. "And here we have milady's eiderdown comforter." He looked strangely as though he were enjoying himself. "Not exactly the Connaught, but it will suffice, don't you think?"

She smiled inwardly at his enthusiasm. It wasn't what she had been expecting from him. "I'm speechless with admiration. I didn't think you had it in you to be practical."

"Well, as you can see, I'm not just another pretty face," he said, beginning to arrange the bags on the floor in front of the bench. "I have brains as well as beauty."

"And we've already established your modesty." She chuckled.

"Quite," he agreed, absorbed in his task.

She watched as he vigorously fluffed the burlap bags, then spread the canvas neatly over the makeshift bed. "Mark," she asked curiously, "are you part British or something? I've never heard anyone say 'quite' like that—except maybe Cary Grant."

He stopped working for a moment and looked at her with an amazingly boyish grin. "I did spend several years in London, but"—his voice dropped to a confiding whisper as he glanced around in an exaggeratedly conspiratorial fashion—"if you want to know the truth, ninety percent is pure affectation." As she laughed in delight, he added hopefully, "If it would help I'll start saying 'y'all' and wear cowboy boots and chew tobacco."

"Good Lord, no!"

"Oh, well," he said, unable to keep the relief out of his voice. "Perhaps it's best. The vernacular and boots I could manage, but I'm afraid the chewing tobacco would prove more difficult."

"I can imagine." She smiled.

"I can't," he muttered, grimacing in distaste. "Now, if you're ready, your bed awaits."

Maggie looked from the pallet to Mark, then back to the pallet. "Mark," she said hesitantly, "you wouldn't . . . I mean, tonight while I'm asleep, you won't . . ."

"Maggie," he chided, shaking his head, "how can you even ask? I may have a few eccentricities, but necrophilia is definitely not one of them. You can go to sleep and dream the sweet dreams of the righteous without fear. I promise I won't touch you. At least," he added with a wicked grin, "not until you're awake."

"Mark!"

"Just teasing, love. Now, come to bed." His smile became curiously wistful. "That sounds nice, doesn't it. Come to bed, Maggie."

What a complex man, she thought as she removed her shoes, shifting her eyes to the floor when he began unbuttoning his shirt. She could never tell when he was acting and when he was serious—that is, if he ever *were* serious. Maggie had the feeling that sobriety was one of those eccentricities to which he didn't subscribe.

Minutes later, as she drifted off to sleep, enveloped in the warmth of his lean body beside her, Maggie thought how strange it was that she had never felt this comfortable and secure sleeping beside Barry. Then, in one of those brilliant flashes that come on the threshold of sleep and are never remembered afterward, she thought how wonderfully right it felt.

"No!"

Maggie jerked awake as the sound that had been gradually incorporating itself into her dream finally separated into reality. She felt Mark twisting beside her, moaning softly in his sleep. Peering at her watch in the darkness to confirm that it was indeed morning, she wondered anxiously if she should wake him from what was obviously a nightmare or let him sleep through it and wake naturally.

She looked closely at his beautifully shaped features. The confident, almost arrogant look that seemed natural to him was gone, and in its place was a look of such anguish, she simply could not let it continue. She gently touched his face, finding it damp with perspiration.

"Mark?" she whispered softly in his ear.

Jerking his head away from her hand, he mumbled unintelligible, urgent words. Then her hand gently shaking his shoulder seemed to penetrate his dark world, for his eyes flew open suddenly. "Maggie?" he whispered hoarsely, searching her face avidly in the dimness.

"Oh, God!" He groaned, closing his eyes and

pulling her abruptly into his arms, holding her so tightly she could scarcely breathe. Burying his face in her neck, he pressed her lower body close, as though he were trying to absorb her.

Maggie was so caught up in his intensity, the desperation evident in his urgent movements, it never occurred to her to protest. He needed help, and she could provide it. But what started as comfort gradually changed into something far more self-serving. His lips on her neck and face, his hands moving on her body, started tremors of feeling that grew in intensity until her urgency matched his.

She touched his smooth, bare chest with trembling fingers, feeling she was about to make an important discovery. How could simply touching and being touched cause such acute sensation? It was as though all her senses had been veiled. Now, suddenly, the veil was lifted, and she was giddy with the heightened awareness.

He moved his impatient lips to the vulnerable, tingling skin behind her ear, and she arched her neck to the side, helpless against the tantalizing spell of his touch. His long fingers explored her back—caressing and smoothing, and neglecting not one inch of the velvety-soft skin.

His lips moved slowly across her cheek, tasting the warmth. She moved her head toward the magnetic attraction of his mouth, and their lips met explosively, bringing a whimpering moan of pleasure from her, a startlingly earthy groan of satisfaction from Mark. She brought her fingers up to clasp his neck, guarding her pleasure with eager hands, as he caressed the sweet inner parts of her lips with short, thrusting strokes of his tongue.

From somewhere in the midst of the sensual

mist surrounding her, she acknowledged his fingers on the buttons of her blouse and gave a delicious shudder of anticipation. Searching his face as he drew back from their kiss, she found his eyes trained with consuming hunger on the treasure his fingers were revealing.

He finished the last button and slowly drew her blouse open, catching his breath sharply as though discovering something wondrous and rare. The aching intensity in his glazed eyes was the most erotically stimulating thing she had ever experienced. His eyes slid over her swollen breasts, with their provocatively taut tips, his face tense with impatient greed, sending a thrill of longing surging through Maggie's veins. She moaned deep in her throat as his eyes devoured her body, affecting her as more substantial caresses had failed to do in the past.

"God, Maggie," he breathed, his voice rough with desire. "You're beautiful." He seemed crazed, driven by unseen spirits as he lowered his head to her breasts. "So perfect . . . so precious."

He cupped one small, firm breast with his large hand, bringing it to meet his rapacious lips, and sucked the erect nipple deep into his mouth, sending a burst of incredible sensation coursing through her body. Closing her eyes, she threw back her head in exultant delirium. Her body's reactions were suddenly taken out of her control. She was a quivering puppet, sensually arching her hips, digging frantic fingers into Mark's shoulders as an invisible puppet master pulled erotic strings.

He moved to share the bounty of his enthusiastic lips with the other envious breast, removing her blouse with skillful tugs. When she was free at last of the restraining garment, he drew her with slow, deliberate movements to his strong, muscular chest, and the feel of warm, naked skin merging was so blindingly beautiful, so breathtakingly exquisite, she wanted to clasp the sensation to her and hold it close forever.

Sliding her hand irresistibly across his shoulders and down his back, she reveled in the feel of his smooth, strong flesh. She continued her downward path to his lower back, following the ridge of his spine to his lean, hard buttocks, stroking and molding the rounded flesh through the soft material of his slacks.

Her exploring touch brought a deeper, harsher groan from Mark. He sounded strangely as though he were in pain, as he pushed her pliant body urgently to the pallet. He began to kiss the silken softness of her shoulders and neck. Then, moving lower, he teased each tumescent breast with catlike strokes of the moist, warm tip of his tongue, concentrating on the hypersensitive peaks standing sensually erect.

Maggie moaned in disappointment as his mouth left her breasts, then in the same moment gasped with pleasure as he brought his unflaggingly delightful caresses to her navel, his hands on either side of her small waist holding her a willing captive.

With a minimum effort his agile fingers released the fastener on her jeans and slid the zipper down, parting the fabric as he stroked the warm flesh beneath. When the seeking fingers encountered the lace top of her bikini panties, they slid under the sheer fabric without a pause and moved across her slim hips to grasp her warm, rounded buttocks.

His mouth then followed the path his fingers

had blazed. He buried his face in the soft, satiny skin of her stomach while his hand cupped and molded the smooth flesh of her derriere, pressing her closer to his demanding lips.

Maggie's fingers sought his thick blond hair without waiting for a conscious command from her dazed brain. She pressed his head ever closer, her body writhing in unbearable need. She felt she would burst if the incredible mounting tension in her lower body were not assuaged.

"Mark!" she gasped frantically. "Please."

He moved swiftly, rising above her, then lowered his head to absorb the sound of her desire with his hungry mouth. Her tongue sought his, darting eagerly until he mastered the sensuous duel and plunged his tongue intimately into the honeyed depths of her mouth, an erotic mime of the act they were both craving.

Her anguished moan brought his head back so that he could search her bewitched features. "Yes, Maggie?" he asked, seeking permission to continue in a harsh, urgent whisper. His hand rested on her partially bared hip, awaiting a sign of affirmation.

"Oh, yes. Please, Mark," she murmured hoarsely. Then, as he drew in a deep breath and his long fingers began to slide the fabric down, her innate honesty forced her to add, "Mark, you know I don't—"

"I know, princess," he interrupted gently. "You don't like me. Don't worry about it." He looked into her dazed eyes. "Don't you see? It doesn't matter. Right now there are no labels between us. There is only this." He moved to kiss her swollen lips—soft, slow, drugging kisses—leaving her weak with desire, unable to think sanely.

Gradually a combination of sounds crept into their dark haven, disturbing their sensual wonderland. Mark lifted his head lethargically in a distracted acknowledgment of the intruding noise, and at the same time Maggie recognized Henry's excited barks. But there was more—a heavy scratching on the cellar door.

"Civilization intrudes, princess," Mark whispered hoarsely, kissing her lips in a punishingly rough caress.

"What is it?" she whispered, still floating somewhere beyond reality.

Mark sat up, sighing deeply as he clasped his arms around his knees, and looked at her regretfully. "Someone is moving the tree. And as much as I hate to say it," he said ruefully, "the troglodytes must emerge." He picked up her discarded blouse, helping her into it, then buttoning it deftly after a last, lingering touch on her breasts. "Whether we want it or not, love, we are about to be rescued."

He stood, muttering a stifled groan of exasperation as he watched her fasten her jeans and slip into her shoes. Then he moved swiftly to put on his shirt. By the time the light from the opening door flooded the cellar, they were at least physically composed, and the pallet that had been their entire world moments before was once again a stack of burlap bags and a folded canvas tarpaulin.

"Mr. Wilding?" inquired a timid male voice.

Maggie stood still, allowing her eyes to adjust to the bright morning sun, as Mark stepped forward to meet their rescuer.

"Yes, John, I'm here," he replied, evidently recognizing the voice. "What on earth are you doing here?"

"It's your father, sir. He called from Ireland last night and wanted to speak to you immediately."

Maggie followed behind Mark, climbing the stairs slowly, confusion pressing in on her from all sides. Things seemed to be happening so fast. It was just beginning to dawn on her what had almost happened in the cellar, but her brain was too foggy to cope with the thought now.

The back yard seemed to be full of people, but as she watched she realized that there were actually only four men besides Mark's friend. She recognized one as Jake's caretaker, deciding the other three must be neighbors. As Mark conferred with the short, dapper little man he had called John, Maggie stood in the doorway of the cellar, looking around the back yard to assess the damage. Miraculously, except for the magnolia tree and a torn screen, everything was just as she had left it. She had heard of the freakish quality of the winds of tornadoes and was glad this particular twister had decided to leave her aunt and uncle's house standing. She had expected to see nothing but wreckage.

"Hello, Henry," she greeted the joyful dog as he shoved her against the doorjamb in his exuberance. "Yes I'm glad to see you, too, but back off a little and let me breathe." She gave the huge dog a shove. "Where are the others, Henry?" she asked, looking around. But she didn't have to look far. At that moment the whole brood came trooping around the corner of the house, and she breathed a sigh of relief that she wouldn't have to face Uncle Charles with the news of the loss of one of his pets.

Now all she had to worry about was Mark. After what had happened in the cellar, how could she possibly convince him that she wasn't interested in having an affair with him? Her response had been explosive, so there was no way she could say she was not attracted to him. Of course, she thought hopefully, his interest could have been a case of any port in a storm. Now that they were out of isolation, he would probably want to go on to his more sophisticated pursuits.

Maggie turned slowly to find Mark watching her, and the look in his eyes effectively canceled her doubts concerning his continued interest. He said something in a low voice to the man beside him, then walked to where she was standing.

"Well, love," he said, regarding her tense features closely, "it seems our subterranean idyll is at an end." She flinched inwardly at his reminder, looking away as he continued. "John is my father's assistant. When Dad called, trying to get in touch with me, John took it as his sworn duty to find me. Knowing Dad, he was calling to let me know that the trout were biting, but that's not important. What matters is that John got in touch with Jake and, finding that I had left the lodge yesterday afternoon, decided to track me down. After he found my car, the rest was easy. Your leviathan friend"—Mark turned and scowled menacingly at Henry—"led him right to us." He lifted a hand to touch her cheek softly. "The only thing worse than a conscientious assistant is a devoted dog. Next time I promise there'll be no interruptions."

"Mark," she began hesitantly, uncertain of how to begin.

"I have a terrible feeling," he said, "that you're about to say something I don't want to hear. Remember what I told you, Maggie. I don't handle defeat well."

"I'm sorry if I gave you the wrong impression, Mark," she began despite his protests. "Down there in the cellar, nothing was real. It was like you said—no labels . . . just the moment. But now we're back in the real world and I have to remember who and what I am. And what I'm not. I'm simply not the kind of person who can pick up and fly off with a stranger. It goes against everything I believe in." She looked at him, an unconsciously wistful expression in her eyes. "It will be easy for you to find someone else to go with you to St. Thomas, but if I went, it wouldn't be easy for me to forget that I wasn't strong enough to do what I believe is right."

He was silent for a moment, his expression thoughtful, as though he were assimilating her words. "Is it the trip and the fact that I would be paying that's bothering you? Or is it me?"

Maggie hesitated momentarily, then closed her eyes and plunged in. "It's both, Mark. I'm my own person and I pay my own way, yet even if there were no trip involved, I would still say no. You're a very attractive man and it would be too easy to become physically involved with you, but we're so different. We don't think the same way. Our lives are too different, and an affair between us would be a dead-end street."

"What you're trying to say," he said with dry humor, "is that if we slept together, you wouldn't respect me in the morning. I suppose it's no use my telling you that your respect is not my major concern here?"

"Maybe not," she replied, wishing desperately that he would stop dragging it out and simply leave. "But my respect for myself is *my* major concern."

"And making love with me would cause you to lose your self-respect?" he queried softly. For a brief moment something curiously like hurt appeared in his eyes, but before she could grasp its importance, it was gone and the playful twinkle was back. "You may be right, love, but after a night in my arms, I guarantee self-respect would be number two on your list of priorities."

"Mark!" she gasped, unable to suppress a smile at his audacity.

"Okay, Maggie, I'll concede defeat." He paused, a wicked grin appearing on his handsome face, then added, "For the moment."

He turned to pull her toward the group of men, ignoring her attempts to question his last statement. After he had introduced her to John Lowe, who turned out to be an absentminded but sweetly gallant man, Mark turned to speak to the other men. Maggie watched curiously as he joked with them about the tornado. Mark was irrepressible. He seemed totally unaffected by her rejection.

Is that what I wanted? she asked herself reflectively. Did I want to see him touched by my actions? Maggie didn't care for the idea at all. She had said no because it was the right thing to do, not because she wanted to test his feeling for her—which was the proper way to have acted, for evidently Mark had no really deep feelings. He was a self-admitted pleasure-seeker, the total opposite of Maggie's more Calvinistic attitudes.

The men suddenly started to disperse, and minutes later Maggie was standing in the front yard surrounded by six boisterous dogs, watching Mark and Mr. Lowe preparing to leave. As the latter waved before stepping into his small car, Mark approached her again. He pulled a card from his breast pocket, holding it between two long fingers when he stood before her.

"Just in case you have a sudden change of heart, love," he explained, extending the card. "All you have to do is whistle, and I'll be there." His deep voice was confident and amused. As she hesitantly reached for it, he grinned and slipped it inside her blouse, his warm fingers touching the rounded tops of her small breasts. He released the card, stepping back, and they both watched as it fluttered to the ground.

Mark laughed in delight as Maggie raised her eyes to heaven, praying for divine intervention. Then he said in a confiding whisper, "Just as I said—compact, but nice." He stooped to retrieve the card, this time placing it in the pocket of her blouse, then turned and walked to his car, whistling cheerfully and never once looking back to see that she watched until he was out of sight.

Chapter Three

"Maggie! You're doing it again."

Maggie looked up from the ivy that had held her mesmerized, to see Carrel hanging over the side of her cubicle. This month Carrel had decided to be a redhead, and, although the color should have clashed unmercifully with her bright wardrobe, she looked as exotically striking as always.

Maggie carefully measured the exasperation in Carrel's face. Her friend had been watching her strangely all week, as though puzzled by something. "Doing what again?"

"You keep going off into some weird kind of trance." Her blue eyes brightened with curiosity. "What's up, sweetie? That's an 'I've just met an exciting new man' look if I ever saw one. And I see one almost every time I look in the mirror, so I should know," she added with a wicked smile.

"Don't be silly, Carrel," Maggie said, her voice

heavy with scorn. "I was just trying to remember when I last watered Sophronia."

"Sophronia is a ridiculous name for an ivy plant. It should be something . . . something leafier," she complained, momentarily distracted from her interrogation.

"Maybe," Maggie said, chuckling. "But she's used to it now. How would you like it if someone told you your name didn't suit your looks? Would you change it?"

"Oh, no, Maggie," Carrel said, looking at her friend in accusation. "You're not throwing me off the scent that easily. Now, why have you been brooding all week? What happened last weekend?"

"I haven't been brooding," she said firmly, then saw the stubborn set of Carrel's elegantly molded jaw. "Oh, very well. I spent the weekend with a gorgeous, wealthy man who begged me to fly away with him to exciting foreign cities. Now are you satisfied?"

"Well, at least your fantasies have improved. You used to dream about being president of the company."

Maggie laughed. "You mean you don't believe me?" she asked, fluttering her lashes in artless surprise.

"No," her friend replied unequivocally. "It's sad to say, but you're simply too practical for something as delicious as that. Now, tell me what's bugging you. It can't be Dave, for heaven's sake."

Maggie regarded Carrel's face curiously. "Why couldn't it be Dave?"

"Be reasonable, Maggie, the man wears argyle socks!"

"Oh, no!" Maggie laughed in mock revulsion. "The kiss of death."

"Laugh if you like, sweetie, but it definitely shows something lacking in his character—like good taste. I would be afraid for a man who chose argyle socks to choose me, too." Carrel leaned closer over the cubicle wall, her expression earnest. "You see what I mean?"

"No, Carrel, I don't. And that's the way I want it. Somehow, the thought of understanding the intricacies of your twisted brain scares the hell out of me."

Smiling at her friend's rueful expression, Carrel walked around the low wall and sat casually on Maggie's desk, crossing her long legs. "Enough of this drivel, Maggie. Tell me what happened last weekend. You went to babysit with your uncle's mutts and then . . ."

Maggie sighed heavily, leaning back in her padded chair, staring at the pencil in her hand. "Actually, it happened exactly as I told you." She paused, hesitating momentarily, then said in a rush, "A storm came up, and I was trapped in the cellar overnight with a strange man."

"Maggie!" Carrel shrieked, causing several heads to turn in their direction. "That's marvelous! And was he really rich and handsome?"

"Oh, yes," Maggie said emphatically. "You would have flipped over him."

"Meaning you didn't?"

"Of course not," she said, then felt crimson flood her face as Carrel looked at her dubiously.

"My God," Carrel whispered in awe. "Maggie, you're blushing! I've never seen you blush before."

"That's because I don't blush," Maggie said drily, fanning her face with a magazine.

"But you are," Carrel pointed out, her voice puzzled. "What happened, Maggie? I didn't think

49

any man could affect you that much. Your immunity worries me sometimes, but I'd rather see you uninterested than take a chance on getting in over your head. I would hate for some slick white knight to come along and hurt you."

"There is absolutely no chance of that happening, Carrel," Maggie assured her friend. "Mark may have been slick, but he was definitely no white knight. He was the most . . . frivolous, superficial man I've ever met." She paused as she remembered the look of agony that had contorted his beautiful sleeping face, then murmured softly, "At least he was most of the time." She shook her head to clear it of the disturbing memory. "Anyway, I'll never see him again, so there's nothing to worry about."

"Mark who?"

"According to his card it's Marcus Wilding the Fourth. Do you believe that? I've met a few Juniors, but never a Fourth."

"Mark Wilding!" Carrel closed her eyes weakly. "Maggie, you idiot! Do you realize who he is?"

"Is he somebody?" Maggie asked, casually curious.

"Is he . . ." Carrel sputtered. "Do you have any idea how many women would kill to spend the night with Mark Wilding?"

"I told you he was attractive—in an arrogant kind of way."

"Attractive? Dear Lord, give me strength." She looked at Maggie with pity in her eyes. "The man is only gorgeous. And famous. Not just in Texas— I mean *internationally* famous. Mark Wilding doesn't go where the jet-setters go. He goes where the mood takes him, and they follow. He has been linked with practically every movie star and debutante you could name. Don't you ever read the newspaper?"

"Sure, I do," Maggie said, overwhelmed by her friend's outburst. "But I read it for news, not for that garbage. I'm sure if he had contributed something worthwhile to mankind, I would have heard about it sooner or later." She looked at Carrel's exasperated face. "I realize what you're saying, Carrel. And of course I'm flattered that he asked me to go to St. Thomas with him. It's very good for my ego. But even you, moonstruck as you are, must surely see that it wouldn't work."

"St. Thomas," Carrel murmured in a strangled monotone. "He asked you to go to St. Thomas with him."

"Are you all right?"

"Yes," Carrel replied, dazed. "Just let me get the blood flowing again." She shook her head, the long auburn hair swirling around her face, then drew in a deep breath. "You're right, of course, Maggie. Any kind of relationship between the two of you would be disaster. But"—she leaned closer— "a fling, sweetie? Couldn't you have a casual weekend with him?"

"I don't even like the man, Carrel," Maggie said in frustration.

"Maybe not, but you feel something, and don't say you don't. I haven't asked what happened in that cellar, because it's none of my business." She smiled and shrugged as Maggie raised her brows in doubt and surprise. "I have to draw the line somewhere. Anyway, it's not necessary. In the two years that I've known you, you haven't had one single affair—you haven't even been strongly attracted to anyone—and before that, there was the adorable Barry. You've never said so, but I always got the feeling that Barry was no great shakes in bed."

"Carrel!"

"Well, it stands to reason. He was selfish in everything else. Why should he be any different where sex was concerned?" Although Carrel had met her ex-husband only once, it had been enough to convince her that Maggie had had a lucky escape.

And of course Carrel was right about the sex. Maggie's years with Barry had been miserably frustrating ones. But Maggie never allowed herself even to think of the barrenness, much less speak of it. She looked calmly at Carrel's intent expression. "And your point is?"

"I know you were a virgin when you married— you did say that much. Which means that you are thirty-one years old and have never had a satisfying sexual relationship," Carrel said in a purposeful whisper.

"Oh, horrors!" Maggie gasped teasingly, and laughed. "Do you suppose it's warped my personality?"

"Maggie, be serious. The chance of a lifetime has just been dropped into your lap. It doesn't matter that he's not the white knight. I'll bet knights are lousy in bed anyway. The man turns you on. Don't deny it," she said firmly as Maggie began to protest. "And he's very experienced. Just look at all the women he's managed to please. You'd be a fool to pass him up."

Maggie looked at her friend's earnest face and sighed. "I'm sorry, Carrel. I can't do it. I'm simply not the kind of person who can just pick up and fly away with a man I barely know. The whole idea seems irrational—and totally impractical."

"For heaven's sake, where has being practical got you? Maggie, can't you see . . ."

Before Carrel could finish her argument, Dave walked into the office, and his presence sent her swaying back to her own cubicle, but not before she had sent Maggie a look that promised more to come.

Maggie surreptitiously watched Dave walk across the room to speak with a visiting consultant. Carrel's derogatory comments about his choice of clothing meant nothing to Maggie, but she had to admit that something had changed in the way she felt about him. Before, his bland expression had seemed calm and quietly dignified. Now it simply looked dull.

She shook her head, irritated at her thoughts, and turned back to work on her latest account, but the doubts kept pulling her away from her work. Why should a man who had been ideal last week suddenly seem so ordinary?

It didn't take a genius to figure out that it had something to do with Mark. Admittedly Mark was enough to make any man seem ordinary, but Maggie wasn't the type to be attracted by surface glamour, especially not after Barry. It must have something to do with the way she responded when Mark touched her. She had never felt anything close to the sensations that being in his arms produced.

And what if I never feel that way again? she asked herself, shivering as she was shaken by an aching sense of loss. Maggie! she reproved herself, you're turning into a sybarite. Think of all of Dave's good qualities. His sensibility, his forthrightness, his . . . his . . . *dullness*, she admitted reluctantly.

Biting her lip in exasperation, Maggie pushed the thoughts away.

As the day wore on she kept running into Dave. Each time she studied him carefully. His quiet smile and soft voice didn't seem signs of dullness. He really was an exceptionally nice man. Always considerate of others' feelings. Always ready to help when help was needed. Maggie finally decided that she would be a fool to let someone as artificial as Mark blind her to Dave's good qualities.

At five o'clock she saw Dave again across the room. He smiled at her shyly as she stood talking to Marcie, a beautiful blonde who was relatively new to the office. Maggie said goodbye to Marcie and turned back to her desk, pleased that she had come to her senses regarding Dave. As she turned, she saw Carrel watching her once again over the cubicle wall.

"What was Little Miss Muffet after?"

"I don't know why you don't like Marcie," Maggie said. "She's really very sweet."

"She's a dumb blonde, Maggie. And she's too dumb to realize that dumb blondes are extinct." Carrel's tone was rich with disgust. "She acts so helpless. It makes me sick to see someone like her set equality back fifty years."

"Why on earth should you think that?" Maggie asked, astonished at her vehemence.

"Haven't you ever seen her go into her frail little woman act? And she's always so blasted sweet. She agrees with everything I say—with everything anyone says."

"I think you're overreacting. I thought what we all want—male and female—is the right to be ourselves, whatever that may be. Maybe Marcie is just being herself."

"She's as phony as my hair," Carrel insisted, unaffected by Maggie's logic. "Why was she over here?"

Maggie hesitated, unwilling to bring Carrel's wrath down upon her head. "She was so excited, Carrel. She has a very important date tonight and—"

"Don't tell me she stuck you with the Lawrence account!" her friend fumed. "Maggie, for God's sake, why do you let people do that to you?"

"Calm down," Maggie said. "I didn't have anything planned for tonight, so why shouldn't I finish up for her?"

"I simply hate to see you let people take advantage of you. Especially that over-the-hill cheerleader."

"You're just jealous because she's the only other woman in the office who can make the male contingent look up when she walks by." Before Carrel could voice her indignation, Maggie continued. "Carrel, I'm an adult. Sometimes I feel that just because I'm small you feel you have to watch me constantly in case I burn my fingers or something." Her attractive friend shifted uncomfortably. "I appreciate that you care, but honestly, I know what I'm doing. If people take advantage of me, it's only because I let them, and it's something I'll have to work out by myself."

Carrel looked at her thoughtfully. "It's not your size, Maggie. You're just so damned naive." At Maggie's astonished look, she continued. "Maybe naive is not the right word. Maybe it's just that you're too genuine and nice for your own good. I know you can be tough when you want to be. Like last week when Jerry made that snide remark about your needing extra time on the Reynolds account because you're female, you laid him out flat with your sharp tongue. But that same afternoon you loaned him ten dollars, when everyone knows he's the biggest mooch in the office and never pays his debts."

"I know." Maggie sighed. "I've been giving it a lot of thought lately. The obvious answer is that I'm trying to buy friendship by being so amenable, but I don't think that's it. I only allow people to take advantage of me when it concerns something that doesn't matter to me—like the ten dollars or the time it will take me to finish this work. Surely that's harmless."

"But doesn't it make you mad when you find out you've been had?" Carrel asked curiously.

"That's the point. I know beforehand what's happening. It just doesn't matter to me—at least, not usually."

Shaking her head in exasperation, Carrel said, "I was wrong. You're not naive—you're just plain stupid!"

Maggie chuckled as she watched the tall woman gather her things together, muttering to herself in disgust as she prepared to leave for the day. Maggie knew that she was lucky to have a friend who cared so much, but there were some things that she and Carrel would never see eye to eye on. There was a subtle cynicism about her friend that would never find its way into Maggie's easygoing personality.

Feeling the need to stretch her legs before continuing her work, she decided to walk with Carrel as far as the elevator. In the hall she suddenly found herself being hauled behind a massive potted plant, and she looked at Carrel in amused inquiry as her friend indicated the need for silence with a finger to her lips.

"Your sweet, shy ingenue is about to devour Mr. Wonderful," Carrel hissed, pointing to a spot out of Maggie's range of vision.

"Carrel," she began in protest.

"Hush!"

Feeling like an absolute idiot hiding in the anemic shrubbery, Maggie stood silently and watched as Dave and Marcie walked by, their conversation low and intimate.

"I think you'll like it, Marcie," Dave said softly, his voice unnaturally eager. "They have the best food in Dallas, and the band is great."

"I'm sure I will, Dave," Marcie replied in her shy, sweet voice. "I'm just glad I didn't have to stay late on that Lawrence account. It's so complicated, it would have taken me hours."

"I told you Maggie would do it," Dave said smugly, his voice just reaching them before the elevator doors closed. "She really is a good scout. And so reliable."

Maggie leaned against the bright turquoise wall, closing her eyes as the words seemed to echo in the empty hall.

"Maggie?" Carrel inquired hesitantly. "Are you mad?"

"Now, what on earth gives you that idea?" she asked through clenched teeth.

Carrel didn't answer for a moment, then she said slowly, "I know it sounds crazy, but I swear I can see steam coming from your ears."

Maggie opened her blazing eyes and glared at her friend. "Very funny."

"Maggie! I've never seen you so furious," Carrel exclaimed, obviously pleased. "It's wonderful."

"I'm always glad to entertain my friends," Maggie said, turning abruptly to march back into the office with Carrel following close at her heels. "I mean, being such a good scout and all." She walked to her desk, opened her purse, and pulled out Mark's card.

"Maggie, what are you doing?" Carrel hovered over her friend in excitement as Maggie picked up the telephone. "Maggie, answer me!"

"The next thing you hear, Carrel," she said, suddenly feeling exhilaration flood her veins, "will be the sound of an image shattering."

"You're calling Mark!" Carrel crowed triumphantly.

"Quite," she confirmed, grinning as the memory of his deep voice saying the same word floated through her mind.

The phone was picked up on its second ring, and a soft feminine voice said, "Mr. Wilding's office."

"Is Mr. Wilding in?"

"No, I'm sorry, he's not. May I take a message?"

Maggie hesitated. As much as she hated the fact, she had always believed in signs, and this seemed a definite indication that what she was doing was wrong. "No . . . no, thank you. No message." She started to replace the phone but felt it being jerked from her hand by Carrel.

"Tell him Maggie Simms called," Carrel said, then hung up looking at Maggie with a satisfied smile. "Did you really think I'd let you chicken out at the last minute? It's about time you did something that was strictly for Maggie Simms."

"It was a nice thought," Maggie said. "But I'm afraid your gesture was wasted. You see," she looked at Carrel wryly, "he doesn't know where I live or where I work."

"Then let's call back and leave the information with his secretary."

"No," she stated firmly. "If it had been the right move, he would have been there."

"Maggie, that's dumb."

"Maybe, but that's the way I feel." She smiled at her friend. "Don't worry. I've learned my lesson. From now on—no more Mr. Nice Guy."

Concern showing in her blue eyes, Carrel asked quietly, "Are you very upset about Dave?"

Maggie sighed deeply. "Not really. It's just the idea of everyone regarding me as a patsy."

Later, after Carrel had reluctantly departed, Maggie finished Marcie's work quickly, then sat thinking in the quiet building. She thought she had made such giant strides after the divorce, but now she found that she was making the same mistake, only in bigger proportions. Before, it had been only Barry she was trying to carry on her shoulders. Now she was trying to carry all her coworkers.

Carrel was right. It was time for her to change. Her amenability didn't indicate an easygoing nature. It indicated an inability to say no to pushy people.

Maggie had always thought of herself as a strong, practical person. And in some ways she was, but it was neither strong nor practical to let people use her. It showed a weakness of character that was suddenly very clear. And definitely not attractive.

She glanced moodily at her watch, to find it was already six-thirty—time for her to leave before she was locked in. She straightened her desk, grabbed her purse, and walked out of the office to the elevator, still wondering what her first step should be in overcoming her "reliable patsy" image. Something drastic, surely. Maybe she should take a week off, leaving her work for someone else. She was certainly due a vacation.

Maggie walked out the front door of the building, completely absorbed in her thoughts. Whatever she did would have to be totally self-serving. Something that would simply give her pleasure. Something frivolous and superficial. Something . . .

"You whistled, love?" drawled a deep, lazy voice from close behind her.

Chapter Four

Startled, Maggie whirled around to see Mark leaning indolently against the building she had just left. "Mark! How on earth did you find out where I work?" she gasped, confounded by his unexpected appearance. "Don't tell me Jake told you that, too?"

He pushed away from the wall and looked at her astonished face, a smile making his handsome features even more attractive. "As a matter of fact, Jake didn't know where you lived or worked," he said, his lazy, polished tones sounding unaccountably pleasing to her ears. "I had to telephone your Aunt Sarah for that information."

"Aunt Sarah?" She stared in open-mouthed surprise. "Do you mean she tells anyone who asks where I work?"

"Of course not," he chided, his gray eyes sparkling with amusement. "We talked for quite a while before she told me. Being Jake's nephew got my foot in the door, but I think what turned the tide was the fact that I'm young, handsome, and gainfully employed." He grinned as Maggie closed her eyes in embarrassment.

"What you mean," she said, sighing in resignation, "is that Aunt Sarah has been matchmaking again." She didn't wait for a confirmation—she knew her aunt too well to doubt it. "And you just volunteered the information about your being young, handsome, et cetera?"

"It simply happened to come up in the course of our conversation," he said with feigned innocence. "After it did, she seemed only too eager to give me your place of employment. And so, my darling La Fayette—I am here." He looked amazingly pleased with himself, standing before her expectantly as though waiting for her to praise his ingenuity.

"Why?" Maggie asked, shaking her head in bewilderment. "Why on earth would you go to so much trouble?"

"It was no trouble. I enjoyed talking to your aunt," he said, stubbornly hedging.

"But it doesn't make sense. From what my friend Carrel tells me, you have to beat women off with a stick. Why me?"

He moved closer, putting his hand earnestly to his heart, and said in a soft Southern drawl, "Why, 'cuz Ah fancy you, Miss Maggie." Then, with raised brow, his eyes sparkling with curiosity, he added, "You discussed me with your friend— that's an excellent sign. What did you tell her?"

"I told her you were the most impossible, exasperating man I had ever encountered," she muttered through clenched teeth. "Please be serious for one minute and tell me what this is all about."

"I have to protect my reputation, love. If word got out that you had turned me down, I wouldn't be able to hold up my head in the country-club locker room." His exaggerated hangdog look made her want to hit him. He sighed deeply and continued. "Everyone would say: 'Poor Wilding—he's past it now. Just a pitiful shell of a man. A shadow of his former self.' "

"You're crazy!" she exclaimed, torn between laughter and exasperation. "Why can't you give me a straight answer?"

He looked at her thoughtfully, his playful expression fading. "Perhaps because there is no simple answer," he said, his expression serious and, strangely, revealing slight confusion. "If I told you why it's important to me, Maggie, you really would think I'm crazy. Can't we just say that I had a hunch—a hunch that came in a dream—and I need to find out if it means anything."

"I don't think I understand, Mark." His solemn expression made her a bit uncomfortable.

"Neither do I, princess, but I've got to find out," he repeated, almost to himself. Then suddenly the strange mood was gone and he continued in his normal lighthearted manner. "You called me. Does that mean you couldn't withstand my charms—which, of course, are too numerous to mention—and have decided to go with me to St. Thomas?"

"You egotistical . . ." she sputtered, about to deny his assumption, then remembered her earlier decision. Under his curious eyes, she stiffened her resolve, took a deep breath, and said in a rush, "As a matter of fact, I have. When do we leave?"

"That's wonderful," he said, looking honestly

pleased and, to her surprise, a little relieved. "Come. We'll have dinner and make our plans."

Before she could blink twice, Maggie was being ushered to the silver Mercedes he had been driving the day of the tornado. She leaned back against the black leather seat, wondering giddily what she had gotten herself into. Whatever was in store for her, Mark was certainly not giving her time to change her mind.

After settling his lean frame behind the wheel, he started the engine, then turned to her. "Where's your car?"

"It's in the shop," she replied vaguely, still dazed by her actions. "I rode the bus today."

"Perfect. Then we don't have to worry about getting it home. Where would you like to eat? Do you fancy French . . . Italian . . . Mexican . . . Greek? . . ." He continued the list, waiting for her to interrupt when he reached the right one. "German . . . Hungarian . . . McDonald's? . . ."

"You choose, Mark," she said helplessly, unwilling to make another decision so soon. Her last one still loomed enormous on her mental horizon.

Thirty minutes later Maggie knew she had been wise to leave the choice to Mark, for the tiny café they entered was charming. It specialized in expertly prepared salads of every conceivable kind. Pots of herbs hung from the ceiling, filling the room with a piquantly fresh aroma. The tables of dark, heavy wood and the waitresses—dressed as eighteenth-century English servants—gave the room an informal yet exciting atmosphere.

During dinner Maggie gave herself up to the enjoyment of the evening as Mark kept her entertained with a running commentary on the places all over the world where he had dined. His opinions of what he drily described as "the gauche, the gaudy, and the godawful," were outrageous, and her unrestrained laughter attracted the indulgent attention of the other diners. Before they had finished their salads the people from the surrounding tables had joined them in a hilarious game of "Can-You-Top-This?"

The time flew by, and the wine seemed to go as quickly. As they sipped coffee laced with cognac, Maggie felt deliciously light-headed, and showed an alarming tendency to giggle at inappropriate moments. But she wasn't bothered by her giddiness. Nothing bothered her tonight. She was enjoying herself more than she had in years. She didn't have the time or inclination to think of anything beyond the present, postponing all thoughts of St. Thomas and her proposed fling until a more sober moment.

In her enchanted state, the drive to Maggie's suburban apartment was a magic carpet ride. The wind that whipped her hair into frothy curls did nothing to blow away the cozy mist that enveloped her brain.

The vague, careless directions she had given Mark as they drove must have been adequate, for they arrived in what seemed like record time at her apartment. As he helped her from the car, Mark smiled down at her with a gentle indulgence that escaped her completely as she leaned against his shoulder, feeling a delicious sense of camaraderie.

At her door, Maggie fumbled through her oversized purse for her keys, but they seemed to take on a life of their own, scrambling out of reach each time she thought she had them in her grasp. She held the bag open wide, peering myopically into its depths, then looked at Mark, who was waiting patiently beside her. "They refuse to come out, Mark. What shall I do?"

Chuckling quietly, he took the purse from her and said, "You're not stern enough, love. You simply can't let yourself be browbeaten by a set of keys." He reached into the bag and pulled out an enormous key ring, which held a miniature flashlight, an antique brass police whistle, an all-purpose screwdriver, a wooden plaque proclaiming "GREEN PEACE," and three keys. Looking at the bulky assemblage he muttered, "Of course, I can see how this key ring could easily intimidate one, but you'll simply have to show it who's boss." Immediately selecting the right key, he opened the door and ushered her inside.

"Won't you come in?" Maggie murmured in cheerful unconcern as she watched him disappear into her small kitchen. Turning, she softly hummed a half-remembered melody under her breath while she removed her jacket, then sat on the long yellow sofa, relaxing against the back with a contented sigh.

She couldn't quite recall what it was she had disliked about Mark. "I suppose it will come to me tomorrow," she murmured, her eyes closing irresistibly with the thought. Whatever it was, it couldn't have been very important. He had given her the most delightful evening she had known in a long time. She wasn't certain if it was the wine or Mark that had inspired the carefree flavor of the night, but she couldn't find it in her to be concerned about it one way or the other. Possibly it was a combination of the two. Whatever the cause, she had become more deeply enthralled with each word he had spoken. He was the most spellbinding man she had ever been with. As a raconteur, Mark was worth his weight in gold.

Maggie heard the object of her thoughts moving quietly into the room, and opened one eye to find him standing above her, holding a cup in one long-fingered hand. "What do you actually *do*, Mark?" she asked.

"I'm charming," he replied succinctly, setting the cup on the low white table.

"Oh," she murmured, finding nothing strange in his answer. She opened both eyes and regarded his tall frame as he moved to sit beside her. "You're very good at your job, aren't you?"

"Naturally." He smiled lazily. "I'm successful at everything I undertake." Picking up the cup, he held it to her lips.

Maggie obediently sipped the strong black coffee, gazing quizzically at his smiling face. "Does nothing ever bother you, Mark? Doesn't anything ever ruffle your feathers?"

"My dear Maggie," he said, raising one elegant eyebrow. "If one could stretch one's imagination so far as to picture me with something as ordinary as feathers, they would definitely be well-groomed feathers."

Maggie stared in open-mouthed awe, then expelled an appreciative breath. "I guess that's what I admire most about you," she murmured, almost to herself.

"Are you saying you actually admire something about me?" Mark asked, his eyes widening in surprise. "Evidently my campaign is beginning to pay off. Didn't I tell you I would eventually bring you around to my way of thinking?" He looked at her inquisitively. "Which of my many virtues do you find admirable? The perfection of my appearance? My remarkably even-tempered nature?"

"Your diction," she informed him enthusiastically. "You e-nun-ci-ate everything so clearly. It makes everything I say sound nasal and slurred in contrast." She sighed. "It's beautiful."

Mark looked at her blankly for a moment; then his surprised laughter erupted and filled the room with a deep, rich sound so contagious that Maggie joined him, not knowing or caring why they laughed.

Setting the cup on the coffee table, he pulled her into his arms in an exuberant hug. "You're priceless." He kissed the tip of her slightly retroussé nose. "Sometimes, Maggie, I want to fold you away in my wallet so that I can carry you next to my heart and take you out whenever I need a lift." He pushed the curls from her forehead in a gentle caress. "Having you admire my diction was not exactly what I had in mind, princess, but I suppose it will have to do for a start." His large hand slid down her face, exploring her delicately molded cheekbone, discovering the hint of obstinacy in her gently squared jaw, then slipped to her neck, ruffling the baby-fine curls that clung to her vulnerable nape.

Shielded from reality by a warm, alcoholic glow, Maggie snuggled closer in his arms, moving her face against his broad shoulder like a satisfied cat. A contented "M-m-m-m" was her only attempt to hold up her end of the conversation.

As though her murmur of pleasure were a signal, he launched a delightful series of soft, nibbling kisses, beginning on her forehead, then wandering down to her closed eyelids, across her cheek to the sensitive skin behind her ear, then to the corner of her slightly parted lips.

"Mark," she whispered, her husky voice sounding sensual even to her own ears. "Are you trying to seduce me?"

"Yes," he answered softly, without hesitation, his breath against her lips causing them to tingle in awareness. "Am I succeeding?"

Maggie chuckled lazily, lifting her heavy lids to look into his eyes and discovering they had turned several shades deeper, to a glinting steel gray. "You're a devious man, Marcus Wilding the Fourth," she murmured. "But I don't care, because"—she dropped her voice once again to a confiding whisper—"I'm a little tiddly." Bringing her hand to the back of his neck, she threaded her fingers through the thick, springy blond hair and, with the slightest pressure, urged him back to her lips.

But instead of continuing with the aforementioned seduction, Mark lifted his head and looked carefully at her languid features. "And if you weren't 'tiddly,' as you so quaintly put it, you *would* care?"

"Probably," she answered distractedly, staring at his lips in deep concentration as she stroked the muscles of his strong neck. When he remained silent, she raised her eyes to meet his. "Does it matter?"

After a momentary hesitation he said, "No . . . of course not," then lowered his head to kiss her waiting lips, gently at first, then with a growing urgency.

Maggie sighed deeply at the first touch of his warm mouth and allowed herself to be carried along on the sensuous tide. Then, just as she was tightening her hold on his neck, Mark lifted his head again.

"Damn," he muttered under his breath, drawing her head down to cradle it against his shoulder with one large hand. "I must be getting senile."

Maggie raised her head to look at him in puzzled inquiry. "What's wrong?"

"It seems," he said drily, "that at this late stage in my life I'm developing principles." His tone was rich with disgust.

"Oh, Mark," she commiserated, unable to suppress her laughter. "How awful for you."

"The understatement of the year," he muttered, then framed her face with his hands, outlining her lower lip with his thumb as he looked into her drowsy brown eyes. "But don't think this is the end of it, Maggie. Just because I want you sober and aware when we make love doesn't mean I've gone entirely soft in the head. Tomorrow night your tipple will be lemonade, and nothing short of cardiac arrest will stop me—understand?"

"Yes, Mark, I understand," she said, smiling in sympathy. "I'm sure this is just a temporary aberration. Tomorrow you'll probably be back to your old unscrupulous self."

Giving her a brief, hard squeeze, he laughed. 'You're just saying that to make me feel better." He stood, pulling her to her feet as well. "I'd better leave now, before I come to my senses."

At the door he turned to give her a last lingering kiss. "Just to hold me until tomorrow, love," he whispered, tipping her chin with one long finger. "I'll pick you up at three, and Maggie . . . ?"

"Yes?"

"You won't change your mind again, will you?"

His expression was unreadable as he waited for her answer.

"No . . ." She hesitated, then continued. "No, of course not."

He regarded her face for a moment as though trying to read her thoughts. Then, apparently finding what he sought, he nodded and turned to go.

Maggie watched Mark disappear into the darkness, then closed the door behind him, leaning against it to find that, although she was no longer under the influence of the excellent wine they had had with dinner, something more potent was moving in her bloodstream. Something more intoxicating than alcohol.

Before she could follow the disturbing train of thought and examine what was happening to her, the quiet was disrupted by the shrill sound of the telephone, and she moved quickly to stop its insistent ring.

"Hello." Her voice came out dreamy, with none of its usual briskness.

"Maggie, it's me," Carrel said. "I've been calling all evening. Where have you been?"

Maggie's face took on a hunted look at the sound of Carrel's voice. She was reluctant to discuss her evening until her mind was clearer, but she knew from experience that her friend would be difficult to put off. "I went out to dinner. You would love this place, Carrel. Their salads were out of this world and the decor was fantastic. They had hung little—"

"You're hiding something," Carrel said suspiciously. "That's a very sneaky voice you're wearing. Who were you with?"

"What makes you think I was with someone?"

"Come on, Mag, 'fess up."

"Carrel, why do you automatically assume that I owe you an explanation of my whereabouts?" Her voice was stilted in a last-ditch effort to evade her inquisitive friend.

"Boy," Carrel breathed. "This story must really be good. What did you do—knock Little Miss Muffet in the head with a tire tool and steal Mr. Wonderful?"

"Don't be ridiculous. Of course I didn't. I . . . I was with"—she dropped her voice to a barely intelligible mumble—"Mark. Now can I go to bed?" she added hurriedly.

"Did you say Mark?" her friend squealed. "But how? When . . . ?"

"Carrel," she interrupted. "I'm very tired and I'm not going to stay up all night to give you a blow-by-blow account of my evening. Just be satisfied with the fact that everything has turned out the way you wanted."

"You're going with him," she breathed in excitement. "When?"

"Tomorrow at three."

"You can't!" Carrel shrieked.

Maggie held the phone away from her ear, frowning in exasperation at her friend's about-face. "Please explain to me—and even though I'm probably permanently deaf I'll try to understand—why you've changed your mind. You were the one who said I needed this . . . this fling in order to aid my growth as a well-rounded human being. You are absolutely—"

"Your clothes," Carrel said urgently. "You have nothing but those too, too sedate business clothes. You're embarking on an adventure, Maggie. You've got to capture the spirit of the thing. No one, but no one can be adventurous in those things you wear. You always look so . . . so trustworthy."

"I do have other clothes."

"Yes, I've seen them," Carrel said in an offhand way, effectively dismissing Maggie's entire wardrobe. "What you need is an emergency shopping trip. I'll take tomorrow off and we'll see what we can do."

Maggie groaned, seeing herself being backed into a corner. "I'm old enough to choose my own clothes," she complained.

"Age has nothing to do with it. If I leave it to you, you'll end up buying tailored pajamas and a three-button, double-breasted, pin-striped bikini."

"Carrel," Maggie said through clenched teeth, her tone threatening.

"Don't try to thank me, Maggie. You'd do the same for me—if you weren't blessed with the taste of a turnip."

Before Maggie could utter the imprecations that leaped to mind, her enthusiastic friend informed her that she would pick her up at eight the next morning and Maggie not so gracefully gave in to Carrel's cheerful bulldozer tactics.

As she prepared for bed, Maggie was consumed by a feeling of helplessness—a feeling entirely new to her. She was accustomed to taking charge and getting things done on her own. Now she felt she was being shoved along a one-way path . . . a path that led straight to Mark.

Chapter Five

At eight sharp the next morning, as Maggie was making the arrangements for her days off, she heard Carrel's knock on the door. Squaring her shoulders, she hung up the phone and walked slowly to admit her friend, the courageous resignation in her bearing reminiscent of a prisoner facing the firing squad. She opened the door to an explosion of enthusiasm that took her breath away.

For the next four hours she was shuffled from one shop to another, trying on mountains of clothes at each one. Carrel seemed to think Maggie would be changing clothes every hour on the hour. After her friend insisted she buy a microscopic sleep teddy in melon silk with sheer ecru lace and a matching floor-length peignoir, Maggie went into a state of blissful catatonia that insulated her against any further shock. She surfaced long enough to rebel against having her hair bleached platinum blond, but couldn't halt the army of eager experts who creamed, massaged, and manicured her into shape.

At twelve-thirty Maggie looked at her smiling friend across a small table in the tea room of yet another department store. Stunned astonishment filled her golden-brown eyes as she asked, "Do you do this every time you meet a new man?"

"I don't have to, sweetie. I treat my body like the finely tuned instrument it is—for which my men are eternally grateful," Carrel added with a grin. "I don't think you even know that you have a body."

"Oh, I know it, all right. I feed it and bathe it and clothe it. Is all the rest really necessary?"

"That's what I mean." Carrel's tone was exasperated. "You said yesterday that Marcie and I make all the men in the office look up when we walk by. Have you never noticed how they look when you walk by?"

"Me?" Maggie asked, surprised. "You're crazy. When I stand next to you or Marcie, I look like the boy next door."

"You're such a bozo! You think that just because you don't have bazooms that you have to carry around in a wheelbarrow, you're not sexy," Carrel said, raising her voice slightly in her indignation—to Maggie's extreme discomfort. "Maggie, if you dressed to emphasize your sexuality instead of hiding it, you would have men falling all over you. I've seen their reactions when they first hear that husky, bedroom voice of yours. Then they tune in to what you're saying and immediately tune out. They start out wondering what it would be like to undress you and end up wondering if you're a robot in drag—a robot with very dull taste in clothing, I might add."

Maggie listened in unbelieving silence, then shook her head skeptically. "That doesn't make sense, Carrel. If everyone is lusting after my body like you say, why did Dave ask me out once, then switch to Marcie? Was he put off by my business suits, too?"

"If any man is brave enough to get past your sober appearance, your sober brain stops them flat. You act like a damned computer." Carrel sipped her tea, looking at Maggie as though gauging her mood, then continued. "You're a business person first and a woman second. If you really wanted Dave, you would have gone all out to get him, and he knows that. You're the most reliable, efficient sales consultant in that office, Maggie. But when a man takes out a woman he wants someone who sees him as a man, not a business colleague."

"What you mean is a woman has to drool all over a man to keep him interested. I thought these were enlightened times. I thought men and women were eons past the game-playing stage."

"Maggie." Carrel sighed. "You've been out in the single world for two years and you're just now opening your eyes to look at it. Forget everything you've read about the new equality. This is reality. When it comes to men and women and their relationships, things don't change. The games you're so contemptuous of are a part of nature. Look at the peacocks. When a peacock spreads that beautiful plumage he's so very proud of, do you think he's going to look twice at the peahen who says, "Yeah, that's nice, but how are you at building nests?" Of course not. It's the peahen who flutters her lashes and goes weak with admiration that he'll follow."

Maggie toyed with her spoon for a minute, then looked at Carrel's serious face. "Do peahens have eyelashes?" After she laughingly dodged the redhead's napkin, Maggie smiled wistfully and said, "I see your point and I suppose it's valid, but it's still a little disappointing. It seems dishonest to me. If I sincerely admire a man, I want to be able to tell him so without artifice." Maggie crumbled the bread on her plate thoughtfully. "I've seen the eye games. You look a man over in a way that says he's something special and he responds in a similar fashion, but it's not sincere. It's all programmed."

"To you it may seem artificial, but to the people involved it's very real. I'm not suggesting you have to pretend to be brainless like Marcie, but there is a happy medium. It's simply a matter of compromise. You have to give men what they need, in order to get what you need. And like it or not, you live in this world, too. You're either going to have to play the game or sit waiting until you're gray for a man who thinks as you do." Pushing her plate aside, Carrel propped her elbows on the table and rested her chin in her hands. "And now that I've done my bit to straighten you out, tell me everything you left out yesterday."

Maggie began her tale hesitantly, slightly uncomfortable about discussing Mark. She had pushed him to the back of her mind and was afraid of what would happen if she took her doubts out to look at them. Carrel listened with narrow-eyed concentration, avidly drinking in every word as Maggie gave her a carefully expurgated version of the events of the past weekend.

Maggie gave the facts as objectively as possible, and as soon as she had filled her friend in on Mark's sudden appearance the night before, Carrel sighed deeply, envy and excitement sparkling in her clear blue eyes as she lit a cigarette, then said, "He's perfect, Mag. He's just exactly what you need. If anyone can get you to look at yourself as an attractive, sexy female, Mark Wilding can. It doesn't matter that he's not your type—he'll make your femininity blossom so that your knight on a white charger will at least recognize you as a woman when he eventually gets 'round to finding you."

Looking at her friend curiously, Maggie remarked, "That's the second time you've said something about a knight. Do I seem to be looking for something as chimerical as a knight?" She searched Carrel's face. "Do you think I'm being unrealistic about the things I expect in a man? I would hate to think I'm not capable of dealing with a real, live man."

"Damn it, Maggie!" Exasperation was evident in Carrel's voice and the abrupt way she stubbed out her cigarette. "When are you going to stop trying to be Miss Polly Perfect? For God's sake, allow yourself an occasional imperfection. Haven't you learned yet that a perfect person makes all us imperfect slobs uncomfortable? Slouch when you walk, or forget your mouthwash or *something*, but stop trying for sainthood."

Maggie sat in stunned silence, trying to assimilate her friend's forceful words. Do I make my friends uncomfortable? she wondered in shock. Because I want to be the best I can be, do I give the impression that I think I'm better than everyone else? Carrel's softly muttered curse interrupted her thoughts, and Maggie raised her eyes to catch her friend's rueful expression.

"Oh, Lord," Carrel said under breath. "Now I've given you something else to worry about. Maggie, forget what I said. You haven't got time to root out a fault today. It's one o'clock already and you still have to pack."

"Pack?" Maggie stared blankly at her friend; then the present overtook her in a rush, and she opened her eyes wide. "Pack! Oh, Lord, I've got to pack!"

She stood, grabbing her oversized purse, then stopped, perspiration springing out in the palms of her hands. "Carrel," she said slowly, her eyes lowered to the discreet gray carpet, "I've got to pack so that I can fly to a place I've never been to with a man I barely know." She looked at her friend in curiosity. "Are you sure this is me?" Maggie closed her dazed brown eyes for a moment, then opened them to add, "I feel so strange, as though it were all happening to someone else. Are you sure I'm doing the right thing?"

"Yes, I'm positive," Carrel said, grabbing her arm and walking purposefully toward the door. "And you are not going to back out at the last minute. Just pretend he's a dose of castor oil. You need him for your emotional health."

Unexpectedly Maggie began to giggle, relaxing in spite of herself as she thought of Mark's reaction to being compared to castor oil. "Okay, I promise I won't back out, but . . ." Maggie looked at her more experienced friend as they walked. "What if he's . . . I mean, what if he wants . . ."

"Maggie, you baby." Carrel laughed. "Don't tell me you're afraid he'll get you to St. Thomas and start sucking on your toes or something." Carrel shook her head in wonder. "You're so dumb. You spent the night in a dark cellar with the man. He had every opportunity to smear you with jam or any other weird thing that came to mind." She pulled Maggie to a stop and looked at her sternly. "Did he do anything that disgusted or worried you?"

Carrel's pointed question brought a vivid picture to Maggie's mind. A picture of herself lying in Mark's arms. She relived the gentleness of his touch, his delight in her body as he undressed her. She shook her head as a tingling warmth spread throughout her body. Her face was slightly flushed with the sensual memory as she answered softly. "No, of course he didn't. And you're right. I'm dumb."

"That's what I thought," Carrel said smugly, eyeing her glowing features. "Now, get moving or you'll be late."

Carrel's animated—and slightly irreverent—chatter kept Maggie occupied on the drive to her apartment. As they unloaded a trunk full of packages, Maggie wondered for the first time what she had bought. Other than the sleep teddy—which stood out vividly in her mind—she had no idea what the sacks and boxes contained.

"Carrel," she asked suspiciously as they dumped their load on the sofa, "exactly how much did I spend today?"

"Don't worry about it," Carrel said, shrugging with cheerful unconcern. "They were worth every penny. And anyway, I've heard that peanut butter is very healthy food."

"That much, huh?" Maggie gave a long-suffering sigh and muttered, "I just hope you bought something pawnable."

Leaving Carrel to sort out their purchases, she went to the hall closet to dig out her luggage. She carried the two pieces she would need into the bedroom and laid them on the bed. As she began removing a few odds and ends from the pale-blue suitcase, Carrel entered the room carrying a periwinkle-blue silk dress draped across her arm.

She stopped suddenly, looking dubiously at the open cases on the bed. "Maggie, that stuff is awful. It looks like surplus from World War II. If you had told me you needed new luggage, we could have bought some today."

"Thank heaven for small favors," Maggie grumbled. "There is nothing wrong with this. It's good, sturdy luggage. My parents gave it to me when I went away to college."

"That was thirteen years ago, stupid," Carrel said, shaking her head in exasperation. "It's banged up and scarred and it simply doesn't look like it's about to fly away on an exciting adventure. It looks like it's going on a Greyhound to visit Aunt Martha."

"Then it matches me. So if I can go, it can go," Maggie said thrusting her chin forward obstinately.

"Okay, don't get so huffy. I simply wanted you to have a touch of panache."

Maggie looked at her friend, a thoughtful expression on her face. "What if I can't handle panache? Maybe I'm supposed to be the reliable old slippers type. Maybe being a good scout is in my genes."

"That's unmitigated applesauce and you know it," Carrel argued. "Good scouts are not born that way. It takes years of practice. The rut you're in is simply habit, and now you're going to start forming new, less boring habits."

A strange expression crossed Carrel's striking face, and she walked to the window, nervously stroking the silk dress as she walked. She looked out into the courtyard, silent for a moment, then turned to face Maggie. "What I said in the tearoom— I didn't mean . . ."

"Don't apologize, Carey," Maggie interrupted, feeling her friend's embarrassment. "You know you can say anything to me."

"I know. But I wouldn't hurt you for anything in the world." She hesitated, moistening her lips. "It was a case of two neuroses meeting. You're always so careful to examine your motives, making sure everything you do is logical and right. I feel so damned inadequate, and every time you work out another fault, it seems to put me a rung lower on the ladder."

Maggie sat slowly on the bed, stopped in her tracks by Carrel's unexpected confession. "But you're the most secure person I've ever met—other than Mark, that is. You're beautiful and intelligent and witty. For heaven's sake, you absolutely exude self-confidence."

Carrel shrugged her elegant shoulders and sat beside Maggie on the bed. "It's all bluff. Something I began years ago. I figured if everyone thinks I'm sure of myself, maybe someday it'll take root and I really will be." She looked at Maggie as though struck by a sudden thought. "Maybe Mark is all bluff, too."

"No way," Maggie stated unequivocally. "There is no way his confidence is only skin deep. It goes all the way to the bone. He was born knowing exactly who and what he is. And if he occasionally forgets, I'm sure there are dozens of women just waiting to remind him. You'll see what I mean when you meet him."

Carrel stood, shaking away her reflective mood. "I suppose you're right. Anyway, we don't have time to analyze either Mark or me right now. Come on, old girl, let's get moving."

For the next thirty minutes they moved back in time and were teenagers preparing for their first date, giggling hysterically one moment, shrieking in anguish the next. Carrel hurriedly packed the new clothes while Maggie showered and dressed.

Maggie was slipping into honey-colored linen pants when the doorbell rang. All motion in the room was halted abruptly; then they turned slowly to look at each other.

"Do you want me to let him in for you?" Carrel asked, trying very hard to sound nonchalant.

Maggie nodded silently, wiping the palms of her damp hands on her slacks. She watched Carrel leave the room; then, as though in a trance, picked up the short, belted jacket and pulled it on. After slipping into her leather sandals, she moved to the door, pinned a brave smile on her face, and walked into the living room.

Mark was standing with his back to her, laughing softly at what Carrel called her party prattle. Was it only last night that he'd been here in this room making love to her? In her mind he was so separated from reality, she might have only dreamed him. But his tall, lean frame was too solid, too real to be a dream.

As though sensing her presence, Mark turned his head in her direction, regarding her silently. Then he held out one hand to her and the invisible puppet master once more pulled the strings to move her across the room and lay her hand in his.

"Hello, Maggie Simms."

His deep voice sent electric sparks shooting through her, concentrating in a tingling mass in her fingertips. "Hello." The soft huskiness of her voice gave the whispered word an intimacy Maggie had not intended. She wanted to take it back. She wanted to move away and give a new, casual tone to their meeting, but his eyes held her rooted to the spot. The silver sparks radiating from the irises seemed to catch fire while he gazed steadily at her until she felt the silver flame as a physical touch on her face.

Suddenly Maggie realized she had tightened her hold on his hand and was clutching it fiercely. She slid her hand from his in embarrassment, turning her head away just as Carrel's voice penetrated her spell.

"No, really," Carrel said to no one. "Begging won't help—I simply can't stay. I promised my neighbor I would pick up some denture cleaner for her, and it's a treat I've been looking forward to all day."

Laughing softly at her friend's idiocy, Maggie walked to the door and waited as Carrel said good-bye to Mark. She gazed at the pale-green carpet until Carrel was standing before her.

"Maggie," Carrel whispered as she walked out the door, "he's delicious. If I weren't positive he would notice the switch, I'd lock you in the closet and go in your place."

Maggie closed the door, took a deep breath, then turned quickly to lean against it. "Well," she said, intending to sound bright and breezy. Instead she sounded scared and squeaky, so she began again. "Well, Mark, what do we do now?"

Without giving him a chance to answer, she pushed away from the door and walked to the center of the room, talking nonstop. "This is all new . . . at least, the flying away part is new . . . I'm certainly not trying to say I'm a virgin . . . I was married for six years, for heaven's sake, and . . . well, anyway, what I mean is, I've never done this sort of thing before and . . ." Maggie clenched her fists and closed her eyes tightly. "God," she whispered, "please don't let me say, 'I'm not that kind of girl.' " She waited a moment, then opened her eyes, raising them heavenward to murmur, "Thank you," then lowered her gaze to Mark. "I'm ready," she said firmly.

Mark looked at her silently for a brief moment, then smiled a gentle, understanding smile and walked to her. As he enfolded her in his strong arms, she relaxed against him, snuggling into the comforting warmth of his body.

"You poor baby," he whispered against the top of her head. "Don't worry. It will be all right—I promise."

"Oh, Mark," she groaned. "I'm such an ass."

"Yes, love," he agreed soothingly. "But the loveliest ass I've ever seen." He tilted her chin, forcing her to look at him. "Feel better now?"

Smiling up at him, Maggie said, "Yes, thank you."

"Then let's go," he said, hugging her enthusiastically. "Blue skies and excitement are waiting just beyond the horizon, love."

"I don't think my nerves can stand any more excitement," she murmured helplessly as she moved past him to get her purse and the smaller case. Mark followed, chuckling as he lifted her other case, and Maggie thought what an attractive sound his laugh was. It was the last truly lucid thought she was to have for quite a while.

From that moment on things moved too quickly for thought. An enthusiastic young man drove them to the bustling regional airport, where enthusiastic young people behind the counter turned them over to enthusiastic young stewardesses. Maggie suffered their exuberance in silence, smiling indiscriminately and, she feared, somewhat vacuously, growing more and more nervous with each passing minute—all under the smilingly watchful gray eyes of her tall companion.

When, after take-off, the attractive attendant offered them a drink, Maggie's acceptance was comically grateful. "Yes, please. I'll have—" she began.

"Lemonade," Mark interrupted, his voice quiet but emphatic.

Maggie turned to look at him inquiringly. He was leaning back, resting his head against the high-back seat. Glancing at her from the corners of his eyes, his lips softened in a sensual smile, and he murmured, "Lemonade—remember?"

Maggie's eyes widened as she remembered his promise of the night before, and she swallowed audibly before haltingly requesting a soft drink.

"You seem a little nervous, love," Mark said, his tone concerned but his eyes twinkling with mirth. "Is something wrong?"

"No . . . no, of course not. It's just . . ." She felt hopelessly pressured—pressured by all the enthusiasm, by Mark's smiling eyes. "Everyone is so damnably cheerful," she complained unreasonably.

"I'm sorry," he said apologetically, subduing a

grin as her eyes narrowed suspiciously. "I could stand and make a speech on war or famine if it would make you feel better."

Maggie's rude comment on what he could do with his speech was mercifully obscured by loud laughter from the seats behind them, and she hurriedly excused herself to go to the ladies' room.

But the aluminum-walled bathroom did nothing to soothe Maggie's frayed nerves. She felt she had fallen down the White Rabbit's hole, encountering strange creatures in a strange land, with every one of them accusing *her* of being the odd one. It seemed like a well-planned conspiracy to make her feel that, even if she couldn't recognize it, everything happening to her was perfectly normal.

Maggie leaned weakly against the door, the fog that had surrounded her all day lifting at last. This is crazy, she moaned silently. Why am I here? Surely there must be a less traumatic way to break a bad habit. She could have started small and gradually worked her way up to this. A novice climber doesn't start with Mt. Everest, she told herself. He begins with tiny little hills and advances slowly to mountains.

So what do I do now? she asked herself frantically. My silver-eyed Mr. Everest is out there waiting for me to return to my seat, so it's a little late for second thoughts. After all, no one was going to offer to turn the plane around for her. Maybe if she offered to pay for her own ticket Mark would forget his plans for her. Pay for it with what? she thought contemptuously. After that shopping trip, I'll be lucky to have peanut-butter money for the next month.

Maybe I could talk my way out of it, she thought.

But that seemed vaguely dishonest, like breaking a promise or going back on her word. She shook her head, reluctantly rejecting the thought. That was not Maggie's way. So, she decided, breathing deeply in resignation, there's no help for it. I'll simply have to go through with it.

She wished suddenly that she and Mark were alone. When he was holding her everything seemed right. It was only when she left his arms that this affair seemed to go against her nature. This fling business was simply not her style. She had never been impetuous, and action without careful thought behind it was worrisome to her orderly mind.

However, according to Carrel, it wasn't her nature at all, but merely a habit she had acquired over the years. It was all academic anyway, and deciding between the two would accomplish nothing —except to delay the inevitable. She simply had to accept the situation and carry on from there. Having made the decision, Maggie's panic subsided somewhat. She was almost relieved to find no action was called for, as she made her way back to her seat before she could think of another futile argument with which to torment herself.

Mark seemed untroubled by her extended absence. He was still reclining comfortably in the seat with his eyes closed. Maggie quietly resumed her former position, being very careful not to disturb him. Breathing a sigh of relief, she leaned back in the seat, then turned her head to look at the cause of her turmoil.

In repose, his features were even more striking than usual. With a face like that he could have been an actor or model. She allowed her gaze to drift down his broad shoulders and chest. His silk suit fitted like a second skin, perfectly molded to his lean frame. Maggie couldn't imagine him in anything other than the expensive clothing he always wore. He probably wears a smoking jacket when he's relaxing, she thought, smiling inwardly.

"Was it too small?"

His softly spoken words brought her gaze back to his face. His eyes were open, an unfathomable smile causing the corners to crinkle slightly, and he was studying her face. Maggie stared at him, lines of puzzlement appearing on her forehead. "Was what too small?"

He lifted her hand from her lap, holding her outspread fingers against his. Staring at their two hands, he turned them first one way, then another, as though fascinated by the difference in size. Then, glancing up at her face, he said casually, "The window in the ladies' room. I thought perhaps you went in there to climb out the window and escape the ogre." He returned his gaze to their intertwined fingers. "Since you were gone so long, I was afraid you had tried it and gotten stuck. I was just about to ask the stewardess for a blowtorch, when you returned."

"There's no window in the—" she began, then caught sight of the merriment dancing in his eyes. "Very funny," she muttered, pulling her hand away and returning it to her lap.

A loud, cheerful argument broke out across the aisle, and Maggie glanced toward the sound, around at the other passengers, and then back to Mark. "I thought all you wealthy playboys owned your own jets," she said, her voice sweetly sarcastic.

"You're just chock-full of preconceived notions, aren't you?" he asked, looking at her with raised eyebrows. As she had the grace to shift her gaze uncomfortably, he chuckled and said, "Actually, I do own one tiny, little jet, but I didn't think it would impress you, so I let John use it for his trip to Austin. Was I wrong? Would you have been impressed?"

"No," she stated bluntly.

"Good. I'd hate to make a tactical error so early in our relationship."

Our relationship, Maggie echoed silently. Why did he have to say that? If he would just stop making those intimate comments and looking her over like a rib roast he had picked up for dinner, maybe she could at least get to the hotel before turning into a sniveling coward.

But he didn't take his eyes off her. Even when Maggie pretended to sleep, she could feel him watching her, feel that silver flame penetrating her flesh like the rays of the hot summer sun. Throughout the changeover in Miami, he watched —and smiled. When she chattered like a silly schoolgirl, he watched—and smiled. During the drive from the airport in Charlotte Amalie, he watched and—damn his silver eyes—he smiled.

The smile grew to menacing proportions in her frantic mind. In the backseat of the taxi, the evening darkness cast mysterious shadows around his tall figure, and the barely distinguishable movement of his lips as the smile widened sent tremors rippling through her exhausted body. She glanced hurriedly out the window, to find they were climbing steadily up a winding road, passing through what appeared to be a residential area.

"The hotel . . ." The words seemed to stick as her throat closed in a nervous spasm. "The hotel must have a nice view if it's on the top of this hill."

"Hotel?" he asked quietly.

"The hotel where we're . . ." She paused as a new and terrifying thought took hold. "We're not staying at a hotel," she murmured in defeat.

"No, we're not." His voice was almost a whisper.

Their arrival at their destination, the transfer of their luggage, and the departure of the taxi all took place in a blur of motion. Maggie stood dazed the whole time. What's happening? she thought in bewilderment. At her apartment, he had been charming, and so thoughtful of her feelings. Then suddenly he had turned into something out of a late-night horror movie.

She stood in the eerie shadows of the tiled entry hall, oblivious to her lush surroundings, and watched, a chill running down her spine, as Mark closed the enormous front door with a loud, echoing thud, then leaned against it.

"Maggie," he said quietly, his voice serious—deadly serious. "I want you to be comfortable here, but there is one thing I will not tolerate, so listen carefully." His voice dropped to an ominous whisper, and his polished accent became a startlingly good imitation of Bela Lugosi. "Don't ever go into the room at the end of the hall, my lovely. I keep ten of my wives chained in there."

Maggie closed her eyes, inhaling a deep, slow breath, then opened them to glare at him in narrow-eyed fury. "You low-down"—she whispered the words in venomous rage, her voice barely audible above Mark's laughter, as she searched the hall for something to throw—"conniving, misbegotten worm!" She picked up an empty vase and held it threateningly high as she advanced toward

Mark, who was leaning weakly against the door, his large frame shaking uncontrollably. "You did that on purpose. All that silent watching. And that evil smile!"

"Now, Maggie," he gasped, circling around her warily, still laughing. "Be reasonable, love. You looked as though you were about to enter Bluebeard's castle." He smiled at her beguilingly. "It was an irresistible impulse."

"Yes, of course," she said through clenched teeth, not pausing in her vengeful stalking. "That's perfectly reasonable. I understand all about irresistible impulses, you see, because I have one right now. To do you great bodily harm with this vase!"

"Not this vase," he said, stepping forward and effortlessly removing it from her grasp. "It's an antique. Let me find you something less valuable to bash me with." He looked around the room, ignoring Maggie's indignant gasp. "Paul must keep something around here especially for bashing."

"Paul?"

"The owner of this house," he explained, picking up a porcelain figurine, then shaking his head regretfully as he replaced it. "He lets me stay here when I have business in town. Although he rarely uses the house, I'm sure he would miss all of these things. Shall we go into the living room to search for something suitable? What you want is something solid enough to do me an injury, yet not too heavy to lift."

"Oh, shut up," she muttered irritably, the impetus of her anger dwindling, leaving her drained.

Mark looked into her tired eyes and frowned in concern. "You look exhausted, Maggie, and my ridiculous clowning didn't help matters. Would you like something to eat? Or perhaps a hot bath?"

The thought of lying in a hot tub was too tempting to resist. "A bath, please," she said, willing to forgive him anything for a chance to soak away her frazzled nerves.

Indicating a door down the hall, Mark followed her, carrying her bags. She opened the door onto a large, spacious bedroom. He flicked the light switch behind her, illuminating the room and, to her overactive imagination, spotlighting an enormous canopied bed. She glanced away quickly as Mark deposited her bags on the bed, then turned to face her.

"The bathroom is through there," he said, casually waving toward a door. "Paul has an excellent housekeeper, so it should be fully stocked."

Maggie moved to the bed to open her large case and remove her nightwear. She raised her eyes to find Mark leaning against the carved end post, and clutched the flimsy garments protectively to her chest. "I'm sure I'll find everything I need, Mark," she said, moistening her lips nervously. "You'll want to eat dinner now . . ." She paused, her voice fading away to nothing. "Or something."

"No, I'm not hungry either." He walked to the closet, pulling out a pale-gray robe. "I think I'll shower and then—" he stretched, covering an obviously feigned yawn with his hand, "then I think I'll turn in."

Chapter Six

Maggie turned away in frustration, walking into the bathroom and locking the door behind her. Her time had run out, and there was no use trying to postpone the inevitable.

Moments later she stepped into the huge sunken tub, paying little attention to the elegant fixtures. One thing and one thing only occupied her mind—Mark. Mark leaning against the bedpost. Mark stretching his lean body, watching her intently.

Damn him! Why couldn't he have let her slide into it last night, when her doubts had been temporarily subdued? Why drag it out until her nerves were stretched to the breaking point? Why . . .?

Hold on a second, Maggie, she cautioned herself. It was grossly unfair to blame Mark for her troubles. Coming with him had been her own decision. It wasn't his fault that she had lost her nerve at the last moment. He had no idea what had motivated her decision to come. Not that the reason mattered now, she thought. She was here, and she was adult enough to accept the consequences of her actions—wasn't she?

Maggie stood and stepped purposefully from the tub wrapping a bath sheet around her dripping body. "Okay, girl," she muttered, briskly rubbing her skin dry, " 'If it were done when 'tis done, then 'twere well it were done quickly.' " Good grief, she thought with a brief return of her normal good humor, she had chosen the wrong play for a quotation. *The Comedy of Errors* would have been much more appropriate than *Macbeth*. She slipped into the skimpy teddy and shrugged on the matching peignoir, then turned slowly to look into the mirror lining one wall.

"Oh!" she gasped, sucking in her breath in horrified amazement and closing her eyes weakly against the reflection. That barely dressed female couldn't be Maggie Simms. Maggie was brushed nylon and cotton. She would never be able to carry off this masquerade. Opening one eye, she peeped hopefully at the image in the mirror—but it remained unchanged.

Flopping down on the satin-covered vanity stool, she nibbled thoughtfully at one neatly manicured nail, glancing occasionally over her shoulder to reconfirm her first impression. "Of course," she murmured quietly, "it doesn't really matter what I'm wearing. It will all come off soon enough anyway." But somehow the thought brought no comfort at all, and confused heat flooded her body. Why couldn't she have a figure like Carrel's? With a body like her friend's, maybe she could have carried it off. But her own was so . . . so inadequate.

"But then," she sighed, "he's already seen most of it. It's not like he's going to take one look at me and shudder in revulsion." Maggie leaned forward, propping her elbows on her knees and resting her chin in her palms. "But we haven't made love. What if nothing happens? What if I really am a cold fish?—uninspiring, Barry used to call me. What if . . . *hic.*" She stopped abruptly, her eyes taking on a harried look as the hiccup shook her body. "Oh, no, please. Not *now.*"

Since childhood Maggie had fought a losing battle against this humiliating affliction, and as a teenager she had suffered agonies over the frequent attacks. Later the spells diminished in frequency and she learned to anticipate the diaphragm spasms, controlling them somewhat with deep-breathing exercises. Today she had been too distracted to give a thought to the possible results. It had been years since her last attack, so that Maggie had been lulled into a false sense of security. Once the hiccups began, she knew she would have no relief for at least twenty-four hours. No remedy, no matter how drastic, had been able to help her after their actual onset.

"That's all I . . . need," she whispered despairingly. Out of self-defense she had taught herself to hide the effects of an attack, frequent pauses in her speech the only outward sign of her inward distress.

"Maggie, love." Mark's voice came through the locked door, causing her to jump skittishly. "Are you going to come out tonight or were you thinking of taking a lease on the bathroom?"

Maggie walked to the door and leaned her forehead against it weakly. "Mark?" she whispered hesitantly.

"Yes, love?"

"Mark, I'm scared."

"But there's nothing out here to frighten you, princess," he said gently. "Come out and we'll talk it over."

Maggie sighed heavily. "Mark?" she whispered again.

And again he replied, "Yes, love," this time with a hint of laughter in his voice.

"Will you . . . walk to the other side of the room before I . . . come out?

"Certainly," he replied. Moments later he added, his voice fainter, "You can come out now, Maggie."

Unlocking the door, she opened it and peered hesitantly into the now dimly lit bedroom. Mark was nowhere to be seen. Puzzled, she stepped into the room to look around, whirling in fright when she heard the door slam shut behind her.

"Mark!" she gasped. "You said you would stay . . . on the other side of the room."

He was standing with his back to the bathroom door, staring at her scantily clad body. "I lied," he stated offhandedly. "Lord, don't you look beautiful in that!"

"No," she stated bluntly. "I look like a floozie."

"You look beautiful," he repeated firmly. "Now, what's this all about?"

"Look, Mark, I've been thinking," she said in a rush, wrapping the loose robe around her waist. "I realize I've been unfair to you . . . and I'd like to explain. This whole thing is really rather silly." She smiled nervously, willing him to see the humor. "There is a man in my office . . . whom I was interested in, but he called me a good scout and took out the cheerleader instead . . . so you see, I'm really here because I got tired of my image.

You wouldn't . . . want me on those terms, would you?"

"Sure, I would," he replied without hesitation, moving toward her.

"Mark!" she squealed, backing away.

"I'm teasing, love," he assured her smilingly, his sparkling gaze again drifting down her petite body. "You don't have to do anything you don't want to do."

His admiring stare spoke louder than his words, and Maggie said irritably, "Would you stop looking at me like that? This is not me." She lifted the lace edge of the peignoir, exposing one shapely thigh. "These things are stupid. The robe doesn't even have a . . . tie. It serves no earthly purpose other than to incite a man's . . . lust."

"It certainly works," he murmured, his eyes fixed on the line of her slender leg. He chuckled softly when she whirled around and walked a few paces away from him. "You're looking at it wrong, Maggie. What use does a smile have? Nothing except to make you feel good when you wear it and to make others feel good when they see it. And do you ask a butterfly to explain itself?"

He walked to stand behind her, grasping her shoulders firmly and moving her to stand before a cheval mirror in the corner of the room. "Now, look at yourself." He moved his hands down her arms, loosening their hold on the robe. "Beauty needs no explanation, Maggie."

She looked at the dual reflections in the mirror but was so mesmerized by his image, she overlooked the beauty in her own. His blond hair was still damp from the shower, and the gray robe had fallen open at the throat, giving her a glimpse of his broad chest. This was beauty. A harsh, stimulating male beauty that his fine suits subdued.

Lifting her eyes from his chest, she met his blazing eyes in the mirror. "Yes," she whispered. "I see what you mean." Maggie also saw the desire that was raging in his now steel-gray eyes, and suddenly, instead of being intimidated by it, she was overcome by a strange calm. "Mark, I . . ." A particularly violent hiccup took her unawares, shaking her body with its force. Maggie closed her eyes in resignation as Mark, feeling the jolt, looked at her in puzzled surprise.

"Maggie?" he said, turning her to face him. "What in the hell. . . .?"

"It's these damn . . . hiccups," she railed, opening her eyes. "They are the most abominable things. I haven't had them . . . in years, and I had hoped I was cured." Miserable, she leaned her head forward to rest it on his chest. "I had them weekly when I was a . . . teenager. At my first dance, my date had to contend with . . . more . . . more than sweaty palms. I hiccuped in perfect three-quarter time . . . all evening. Every time I got nervous I got the hiccups. And knowing they . . . were coming only made me more nervous."

Mark wrapped his arms around her, pulling her closer to his lean frame, and brushed the curls from her forehead in a gentle gesture of comfort. "Poor little princess," he said, laughing softly. "Shedding your comfortable, well-ordered cocoon to come with me has brought it all back for you, hasn't it?" He lowered his head to kiss her on the cheek. "Don't worry so, love. Everything will be fine. I'll sleep in another bedroom, if you like."

"You would do that?" she asked, raising her head, her eyes widening in surprise.

"Yes, I will," he said, then grinned. "I won't like it, but if it will make you feel better, I'll do it."

"I can't believe it. You came down here expecting to . . . make love to a warm, willing woman and you're not even angry about . . . sleeping alone?"

Mark closed his eyes in frustration at the picture she painted and muttered drily, "Don't press your luck, Maggie. It's going to be tough enough without your reminding me of what I'm missing." He opened his eyes and looked down at her. "And if you don't move away from me soon, all my good intentions won't keep me from kissing you."

Maggie was suddenly conscious of his hard body pressing against her softness. She lowered her eyes and brought her hand up nervously to tease the curling hair on his chest. "I don't see what one little kiss could hurt," she mumbled perversely.

"Don't you?" His voice sounded oddly strained.

"Of course, if you'd rather not," she began. He moved swiftly, and her words were lost in a hard, searching kiss.

Mark raised his head a fraction to examine her stunned face. "Now do you see?"

"Yes," she whispered breathlessly, but stood motionless, unable to break the spell his lips had cast on her.

"The thought of making love with me has put you in a highly nervous state, Maggie," he murmured, caressing the side of her neck with gentle fingers; then he lowered his head to kiss the sensitive pulse point behind her ear. "We wouldn't want to do anything that might aggravate those nerves —right?"

Maggie moved her head to give him access to

the velvety line of her neck and agreed in a soft sigh. "Right."

Sliding his hands down her slim back, he caressed her round buttocks softly, pressing her subtly closer to his hardness. "So we'll have to stop now—right?"

She whispered tiny exploring kisses across his chest, nuzzling the V at the base of his neck. "Right," she murmured against his throat.

Drawing a deep, shuddering breath, Mark raised his hands to grasp her shoulders firmly, holding her away from him. "Maggie," he said firmly, "you're sober now—I made sure of that. So any decision you make will be a rational one." He looked deeply into her dazed eyes. "If you want me, I'll stay. If not, I have to know now, before this gets beyond my control." And with those words he threw the whole thing squarely in Maggie's lap.

But Maggie didn't want to make a rational decision. She wanted the delicious sensations to continue until her body took control of her actions without giving her a chance to think. He was forcing her to consider the situation sanely. And, unreasonably, she resented his interference.

Maggie shrugged off his hands and moved away from him to stand at the window. All right, she told herself, think. Study your alternatives. Confused, she leaned her head against the cool glass and suddenly, as though it were written there in the bright, star-filled sky, she knew there were no alternatives. She wanted Mark more than she had ever wanted anyone, had wanted him that way since the night in the cellar, but she had kept the knowledge from herself, shoving it away as foreign to her. She knew now, without a doubt, that with Mark she would come to know fullfillment for the first time. And, greedily, she was going to grasp that with both hands.

Drawing in a soft, shivery breath, she stepped away from the window and walked to the bedside table to switch off the lamp, throwing the room into soft, moonlit darkness. She heard Mark's sharply indrawn breath and felt his piercing stare as the silk robe fluttered to the floor.

She walked slowly across the room until she stood before him. A streak of moonlight fell across his face, casting soft shadows on his tense features. Stretching out her hands, she confidently loosened the tie of his robe, then spread her fingers on his chest, moving them slowly, deliberately upward to push the soft garment from his shoulders.

A groan from deep within his chest broke Mark's statuelike stillness, and he clasped her roughly to his naked chest, wrapping his long arms around her, his hands caressing her frantically, pressing her closer and ever closer. "My God," he rasped. "I thought I was going to have to get down on my knees and beg." He framed her face with his hands in a rough caress, holding her face to the faint light, forcing her to look into his eyes. "And I would have. Never doubt that, Maggie. After I kissed you, there was nothing on earth that could have gotten me out of this room tonight."

The intensity, the urgency in his voice was shockingly raw. This wasn't the lazily laughing Mark she had come to know. She would never have believed she would see such depth of emotion in him. Something was very wrong. Something in his voice went against the easygoing nature Maggie had ascribed to him.

But before she could pursue the puzzling thought

she felt his hands slide to her shoulders to untie the narrow bows; then the wisp of fabric slipped down her body in a silken caress. He took a step backward, releasing her reluctantly, and explored her naked loveliness with hungry eyes. She felt his scorching gaze on her small, rounded breasts, heard his ragged breathing as her nipples hardened into taut peaks under his concentrated stare. Then his eyes glided down past her trim waist and gently curving hips to the curling triangle of hair that guarded the center of her awakening passion.

Maggie stood perfectly still, reveling in his rapt survey, feeling long-repressed desires surge to the fore. She was primitive woman, born especially for this moment of revelation. Her eyes were filled with new, indescribable yearnings as she took in the strength of his shoulders, the symmetric beauty of his chest, with its mat of curling hair that narrowed to a slender trail down the flat plain of his stomach, then spread to embrace his hard, aroused masculinity. She stared unashamedly at him, sucking in her breath as she saw the athletic strength of his thighs, the lean grace of his hips.

As though the exquisite torture had broken all restraints, he pulled her urgently to him. She felt the thunderous pounding of his heart against her naked breasts, heard his harsh, labored breathing in her ear, and the knowledge that she could affect him so deeply sent her mind whirling giddily.

Bending abruptly, he lifted her high in his arms, a barbarian triumphantly claiming his plunder, and walked to the bed to lay her gently upon it. With one knee pressing into the bed, he stretched out a hand to stroke her cheek. "This is the picture

I couldn't get out of my mind," he whispered hoarsely. "Your body gleaming like ivory satin in the darkness."

Maggie lay trembling, waiting. Aching for his body to cover hers. Her breathing came in short, shallow gasps as his words flowed through her veins, hot and heavy like an aphrodisiac. She moaned in hungry impatience and reached up to pull him to her.

Giving in to the pressure of her hand on his neck, he laid agonizingly sweet kisses on and around her aching lips. "Is this what you want, Maggie?" he whispered, punctuating the question with another brief kiss.

"Please, Mark," she murmured, pleading for the solid feel of his mouth on hers.

"Easy, princess." Lying full length beside her, he stroked the side of her neck. "Let it come sweet and slow. We've got all the time in the world."

Sweet and slow. Slowly, he eased her into a fascinating new world of pure sensation, sending shafts of sharp, electric desire pulsating through her body. His hands and lips found all the secret places, and, sweetly, she yielded to the magic of his touch.

His long fingers glided with fairy lightness down her body, learning the rounded curves of her breasts, the silken length of her thigh, and Maggie moved sensually under his touch, shifting her body to meet his hands, his lips as he began an exhilarating symphony of movements. He made love to her breasts, first teasing the hard tips with circular strokes of his warm, moist tongue, then sucking them deep into his mouth, releasing one to taunt the other. He smoothed the soft inner flesh of her thighs with deft strokes, wordlessly urging her to part them to facilitate his erotic play. She writhed with a frustrated longing for his touch at the center of the pulsating intensity, moaning deeply when he moved his hands over her hips to clasp her buttocks firmly with both hands, squeezing and kneading the flesh in urgent, sensual rhythm.

Just as the fire he had kindled in her loins threatened to rage out of control, just as she felt she could no longer contain the fierce pleasure, he pulled her to him, molding her trembling softness to the long, hard length of his body. As he pressed her close, she felt alive as she never had before, every inch of her flesh tingling with sensation.

Her breasts met his chest, the taut nipples discovering the smooth skin beneath his mat of curling hair. She moved her body slowly, her stomach sinuously stroking his. Then they lay for soul-shaking moments, heated flesh meeting heated flesh, undulating feverishly in an erotic, naked pas de deux.

Then, as though their minds had touched as intimately as their bodies, she lay back against the silk sheet while he rose above her, entering her with a swift, sure stroke. She moved to greet his long-awaited possession, feeling him hot and hard between her thighs, gasping with unbearable pleasure as she felt that warmth reach deep within her.

"Magic, Maggie," he said in an urgent whisper, his movements asking—demanding—that she meet each thrust with an ardor as fierce as his own.

Maggie gripped the hard muscles of his shoulders as the pressure in her lower body mounted incredibly. Just as she felt she could not bear one second more without screaming, she heard a harsh, pagan cry from deep inside Mark and, as though the discovery of his delight had shown her the way to her own, she felt rippling, sizzling waves of pleasure lift her into an explosively violent climax and release her gently into peace.

Maggie lay in the darkness, staring at the shades of gray and black in her charcoal-drawn surroundings. She turned her head languidly, a delightful floating sensation pervading her body, leaving her with the feeling that everything was happening in slow motion. She looked lazily at Mark's face, memorizing every detail from his strong brow to the silver eyes that glinted in the dark, watching her closely as though trying to gauge her emotions, to the small cleft in his aristocratic chin.

"You wanna suck on my toes?" she murmured, her speech slow and slightly slurred.

His shout of laughter shook the bed, filling the room with the sound of his startled pleasure. He hugged her to him exuberantly. "Oh, love," he sighed, closing his eyes tightly. "Will you never cease to surprise and delight me?" He opened his eyes and held her chin in one large hand. "I'd be happy to nibble on your toes if you have your heart set on it."

Turning her head to kiss the palm of his hand, she explained. "Carrel thought I was silly to worry about what would happen here tonight. She said you'd had every opportunity to smear me with homemade jam while we were in the cellar if that was what you wanted. She was right. I was silly to worry." Maggie glanced up at his face, moving to lay a soft kiss on his firm, warm lips. "Mark?"

"Shh," he hushed her, grinning devilishly, his eyes closed. "I'm still visualizing the removal of the jam."

"Mark!" she gasped laughingly, pulling back to look at him. "You're a hedonist. But that's exactly what I mean. I can't think of a thing you could do to me that I wouldn't adore."

He chuckled softly. "You mean I didn't have to hide all the orgy apparatus?"

"Orgy?" she asked, scrambling to her knees, her eyes widening in curiosity. "Have you really had orgies?"

With cunning swiftness, he pulled her on top of him, nuzzling her neck playfully. "Not until tonight, princess."

"Are we going to have an orgy?" she asked, unconcerned, as she angled her head to give him access to the full length of her neck.

"We're having one now."

"Now?" she asked doubtfully. "I thought an orgy was louder. You know, with various and assorted bacchanalia, lots of serious debauching, and—"

"I hate to interrupt you in mid-debauch, love, but the correct definition is uncontrolled indulgence in any activity. I plan on indulging in a particularly delightful activity tonight"—his voice dropped to a husky whisper—"And I lost what little control I had the minute your robe hit the floor."

"Oh, Mark," she sighed, wrapping her slender arms around his neck and hugging him in an excess of unrestrained joy. "It was lovely, wasn't it? It was the most . . ." She paused, jolted by an unexpected thought. "Mark! My hiccups are gone. You cured me. Even the doctors weren't able to get rid of them that quickly. You're wonderful!"

"I must say, you're a little slow," he said, smiling at her enthusiasm. "Most people come to that conclusion a lot sooner. But I'll forgive you, because"—he slapped her gently on the derriere—"you've got such a cute fanny.

"Now," he said, rolling over to gently press her body into the soft bed, his voice dropping to a tantalizing whisper, "finish what you were saying about how lovely it was being in my arms." But before she could utter a word he lowered his head, and suddenly bacchanals seemed tame sport as her lips met his in a breathless rekindling of passion.

Chapter Seven

A butterfly lit on her cheek, and Maggie smiled. It was a tiny, pale-yellow butterfly that fluttered a soft caress, then, having taken the time to greet her, flew away to take care of other, more pressing butterfly business.

Maggie lifted her hand to touch the still-tingling skin but found it captured by strong, lean fingers. She opened her eyes slowly, looking at the face of the man lying close beside her on the pillow. "Mark," she murmured, smiling as memories of the night before flowed through her, warming her. "You were the butterfly."

He halted the process of kissing each knuckle to look at her quizzically, his eyebrows drawn together, almost meeting. "I've always considered myself more of a daddy longlegs, but if you want me to be a butterfly, I'll do my damnedest."

Laughter bubbled up inside her. Grasping his

face with both hands she placed a frim, smacking kiss on his lips, then scrambled from the bed and opened her arms to the world. "I can fly," she laughed, whirling around in delight, then looked back at his reclining figure. "What did you do to me? Why do I feel champagne bubbles in my veins and sunshine coming from the inside out?"

Rising from the bed he took a deep, pleasurable breath, as though he too found the very air intoxicating. He walked to her, putting his arms around her bare waist, pulling her close. "I'm not going to take the rap for this one, sweetheart," he said in a very bad imitation of Humphrey Bogart. "It was you," he whispered. "You cast a spell, sang your siren song, and I'm helpless." Sliding his hands to her ribs, he lifted her high in the air and held her there, smiling complacently. "And now you're helpless, so you know how I feel."

"Put me down," she said, laughing.

He looked at her smiling face for a moment as though considering her request, then shook his head slowly in regret. "No, I'm sorry, I can't. After careful consideration I've decided I like you dangling before me. Now, any time I want to nibble on your . . . belly button"—he ducked his head to demonstrate his point, accompanied by her squeals of laughter—"I can. Yes, now that I come to think of it, this is very convenient."

"Marcus Wilding," she said, swallowing her laughter in gasps, struggling for a stern expression. "If I were standing on the floor I would have great difficulty using my knee effectively. But from this position? . . ." She looked down suggestively.

"That was truly a low blow," he reprimanded, setting her gently on the floor. "If I weren't so wonderfully magnanimous I'd make you pay for that one."

"Why, you pompous . . ." she sputtered.

"Temper, temper," he murmured, walking to the window. He moved the curtain aside, and the brilliant sunshine fell on his naked body, burnishing the strong flesh, giving it a deep golden glow. "Look at the world, Maggie," he said, his voice full of a curious, childlike wonder. "It's laughing. Not a silly little giggle, but a marvelously joyous belly laugh. It's out there waiting for us to join it. Let's—" He turned to catch her eyes on him as she memorized the sleek lines of his body. "Like I said"—he paused to clear his throat—"the world can wait." And he walked slowly toward her.

"Now, on your left, ladies and gentlemen, you'll find picturesque, bare-chested crewmen loading their picturesque cargo into picturesque leaky boats. And, of course, here"—Mark gestured to the left—"we have three thousand cruise ships— each and every one of them disgorging their load of"—he paused as a man with a camera around his neck not-so-gently elbowed him aside—"charming tourists."

Maggie giggled at his disgruntled expression, then sobered quickly as, with arrogantly raised brow, he commanded her attention for the rest of his lecture.

"If you'll listen closely you'll catch the beautiful calypso rhythm of the lilting down-island patois."

A loud voice floated across the crowd of rushing tourists to once again interrupt Mark's lecture. "So I says to George—who the hell cares, George?"

Roaring laughter greeted the comment, then the voice was once again lost in the crowd.

Maggie looked up at Mark with an ingenuous expression on her face. "Yes, I see what you mean. There is a kind of rhythm to it."

"Maggie, love," he said, smiling evilly, "how would you like to find yourself dangling in midair again?"

She laughingly ignored his threat as he pulled her along the busy waterfront street. The shops that lined it were delightful, carrying everything from Louis Vuitton luggage to Miss Piggy T-shirts. When they paused briefly to sample pan-fried chicken and a deliciously spicy homemade drink called maubey, Maggie found that the friendly islander who served them quickly, then bent again over the small brazier, did indeed have a beautiful, lilting accent. Mark looked down at Maggie with a smug "I told you so" smile before they walked on.

As they returned to the tiny car that also belonged to their absent host, Maggie found herself smiling at nothing. A deep contentment—no, contentment was too bland—an effervescent joy had filled her since she had awakened to Mark's kiss. She was like a teenager in the throes of her first passion.

Maggie looked at his strong, finely etched hands on the steering wheel as they drove through the labyrinth of roads that wound along the resort-filled coast. His hands should be carved in wood, she thought, only half listening to his explanation of the socioeconomic structure of the island. When she first met Mark she would have thought marble more elegantly appropriate to his character. But now she knew that stone was too cold and hard to do him justice.

With a small smile she admitted to herself that she had a full-blown crush on Mark. How could she not? He had brought her to life. He had given her a knowledge of herself that had always escaped her. She knew fulfillment at last, and she reveled in it.

But Maggie also knew that their closeness, the magical quality of their interlude, couldn't last beyond the Dallas–Fort Worth airport. The dream would end come Monday, when reality would remove the misplaced stars from her eyes. But somehow, knowing that it was a fantasy, that it wouldn't hold up to the bright lights of the real world, didn't diminish the wonder of what she felt for him right now.

Today, all through the day, she had felt the warmth growing steadily inside her. Viewing the lovely Brigadoonish island of St. John from the deck of a sailboat, swimming in the sparkling turquoise water—with Mark outlandishly ogling her brief maillot—and even waiting in a small café for him to complete his business, she had felt it burgeoning. So now, she felt she would burst any minute from the sheer pleasure of his company.

"Was it my description of the rum-making process that lost you? I can't actually hear you snoring, love, but I'd swear you're asleep."

Mark's deep voice broke into her reflections, and she glanced at his face to find him staring at her inquiringly. *He is such a nice man,* she thought, staring at his face. She smiled as she thought of the scathing remark he would make if she dared suggest aloud that he were anything as unexciting as nice. So she simply said, "I like you, Mark."

Pulling the car over to the side of the road, he

stared at her, a curious intensity filling his face, changing the atmosphere in the car. He reached out slowly to touch her face, a gentle stroke on her cheek. "It's a start," he whispered softly. Closing his eyes tightly, he repeated with a strange fierceness, "By God, it's a start." When he opened his eyes again the intensity was gone, replaced by silver sparks of amusement. "Did I or did I not convert you, love?"

Maggie shook her head dizzily, forcing herself to keep pace with his quickly changing moods. She would save the memory and examine it later. "I wouldn't call it converting," she said, chuckling. "I would call it brainwashing."

"I refuse to argue semantics with you. It's not important anyway. What is important"—he leaned over to give her a brief, hard kiss—"is the fact that once again I'm victorious."

"And once again your humility is inspiring to witness."

"Quite."

Their laughter filled the car, floating out into the growing darkness as they drove through the narrow, winding streets to return to their borrowed haven. Mark let Maggie out at the front door while he parked the car. She entered the dim hall remembering how spooky the shadows had looked the night before. Glancing around, she suddenly realized the only rooms she had seen clearly were the bedroom and bath. And those two rooms certainly didn't have the look of a tropic hideaway. There was not a stick of rattan in sight, and no potted palms to bring the lush scenery indoors.

Maggie was walking toward the living room to explore when she heard the front door close. She looked back over her shoulder and saw Mark leaning against the door as he had the night before. Once again his mood had changed. He looked at her without speaking, the sensual vibrations filling the air between them with sizzling sparks. Without a word he quickened her pulse rate, making her come vibrantly alive. Obeying his silent command, she began to walk toward him.

"It's been years, Maggie," he whispered when she stood before him. "No—it's been eons—since I felt your magic."

"Yes," she murmured in agreement.

Without fuss or pretension he put his arm around her shoulder and they walked to the bedroom, neither finding any need for words. Inside the bedroom he picked her up in his arms to carry her to the bed.

They came together as though they had been lovers for years, each meeting the other's needs instinctively in a warm, wonderful pleasuring that was like nothing Maggie had ever felt. It was like seeing a light at the end of a tunnel. Like suddenly finding yourself in familiar territory after being lost. It was like coming home.

Later Maggie lay in the curve of his arm, listening as his breathing returned to normal. She had been more deeply moved than she dared admit. Something extraordinary had happened to her. Something that would take a lot of soul-searching to explain. She couldn't—wouldn't—face it now. Looking through the darkness at his strong face, she kept her voice carefully casual as she asked, "Tell me about your life, Mark. I know almost nothing about you."

"There's really not much to tell," he answered slowly as though he too were having difficulty coming back to earth. "My mother died when I was five, and old Marcus, my grandfather, raised me. When I was fourteen he started grooming me to take over his empire—a job for which I was and am totally unsuited. But he wouldn't believe that, so when he died I inherited the whole mess. I manage to ignore it most of the time, but occasionally—like this weekend—I have to play tycoon. The rest of my time is spent avoiding anything that sounds like work," he finished drily.

"Did you never want to marry?"

"I always considered myself too young to marry," he said facetiously.

She laughed, watching the shadows on his face change when he smiled. "How old are you?"

"Thirty-eight."

"That's too young?"

"I always thought so," he said, then grabbed her hand to kiss the back with exaggerated continental elegance. "But if you'll have me, my lady, I promise to change my dastardly ways."

Maggie laughed and playfully punched his shoulder, unaware that he had flinched when he heard her laugh. "I ought to take you up on that just to teach you a lesson," she said, kissing the spot she had assaulted. Remembering his earlier words, she added, "You said your grandfather had raised you. Where was your father during all the grooming?"

It was a moment before he spoke, his voice strangely stiff when he said, "He was there, but he wasn't *there*, if you know what I mean. Dad was always a little vague, especially after Mother died. I don't think he considered himself a fit guardian. Actually, Jake was more of a father to me than Dad or old Marcus." He paused, and his voice took on a lighter tone. "Speaking of Jake, I have a confession to make."

"Confessions already?" she asked, smiling. "Let me guess. You're taking the kids and leaving me for a mezzo-soprano with the New York Metropolitan Opera?"

"That's close." He chuckled. "The truth is, the day that I stopped to ask directions, I already knew the way to Jake's place."

"No!" she said in feigned surprise.

"Oh, yes, but that's not all," he said, trying to sound contrite but not quite succeeding. "There is no lull in the middle of a tornado."

" 'O what a tangled web we weave,' " she quoted righteously, then said, "Mark?"

"Yes, love?"

"I have a confession to make, too." She paused briefly. "I knew there was no lull in the middle of a tornado."

He raised himself on one elbow, surprise showing in his handsome face. "You knew? You little fiend. Here I was feeling guilty for having tricked you, and you knew all along." He looked at her as though struck by a sudden thought. "If you knew, why didn't you call my bluff?"

She was silent for a moment, then said slowly, "I asked myself that same question all last week, and, although I've only recently admitted it to myself, it was because I liked being in your arms. It felt . . . oh, I don't know how to explain it—it just felt right."

"Yes," he agreed, pulling her closer. "That's exactly how it feels—just like the third bowl of porridge."

Maggie wasn't sure she liked being compared to a bowl of porridge, but she knew what he meant.

Being held in other arms had always been "too" something or other. Only with Mark was it just right.

The next day they arose early and Maggie had a chance to view the other rooms in the large house. Someone had obviously gone to great expense to furnish it, but Maggie found it a little formal for her taste. They were served fresh-baked croissants in a small breakfast room—which overlooked the landscaped grounds—by a shy young Puerto Rican girl who came in daily with her mother and brother to keep the house in order. As they ate, Maggie pestered Mark to tell her what he had planned for the day, but he would say only that it was something special, so she should shut up and eat breakfast.

Leaving the car in the garage, they walked down the hill that rose steeply from the harbor. They passed beautifully maintained manors—a legacy of the Danish aristocracy—then pastel frame houses standing all jammed together in a soft rainbow of colors.

Maggie, finally tiring of trying to keep pace with the man at her side, pulled him to a halt. "Mark, dear," she said patiently, "look down at your legs."

Looking down at the limbs in question, he said, "Yes?"

"Now look at mine."

He obliged by staring at her slim, tanned legs below the white shorts. He spent an inordinate amount of time inspecting them before smiling in pleasure and murmuring, "Yes, love."

"I don't know right off what it's called," she said, drawing his attention away from her legs, "but there's an irrefutable law of physics that states that these"—she pointed to her legs—"cannot possibly go as fast as those," she finished, pointing to his.

"The Law of Diminishing Returns?" he suggested, then laughed and hugged her briefly. "I'm sorry, love. I didn't realize I was going so fast. I'm in a hurry to get to the boat."

"The boat? Are we going sailing again?"

"Just be patient and you'll see," he said, smiling mysteriously, then began walking, more slowly this time.

Closer to the shopping district they met early-morning shoppers and enthusiastic tourists. When they passed a tiny old woman with smooth, dark skin, Maggie once again pulled Mark to an abrupt stop. She indicated the ancient woman's armful of packages. "Those things are too heavy for her, Mark. Maybe we should help her carry them home."

"The islanders are used to carrying things, especially the women. She probably grew up carrying baskets to and from the market on her head."

"But not now," Maggie protested stubbornly. "She's too old."

Mark sighed, seeing the sympathy shining out of Maggie's brown eyes. "Oh, very well. I'll carry them for her."

Maggie stayed where she was and watched as Mark approached the elderly woman, who was now struggling up the stairs of a pale-pink house with her packages. At the front door he returned the parcels to her and listened patiently as the woman smiled and spoke in a strange, musical language, the words foreign to Maggie's ears.

When Mark caught up with her, Maggie said in satisfaction. "You see how much she appreciated your help." She looked up at Mark's face, but instead of pleasure at having played the Good Samaritan, his features showed blank astonishment. "Mark?"

"I'm not completely sure," he said in bewilderment, glancing back at the pink house, "but I think she either propositioned me or put a curse on my offspring for the next three generations."

"What are you talking about?"

"That's what I'm trying to tell you. I don't *know* what I'm talking about. At least, I don't know what she was talking about," he said in confusion. "Her dialect was hard to understand, but I could swear I heard her say something about my 'increase.' "

"And you think she put a curse on them. Now, why on earth would she curse them for three generations?" Maggie asked incredulously, her laughter at the stunned look on his face threatening to spill over at any second.

"I don't know," he said irritably, still glancing warily at the pink house. "Perhaps that's when the warranty runs out."

At that, Maggie could contain her laughter no longer. She leaned against Mark, doubling over helplessly as he looked on with a sour expression. "Oh, Mark," she gasped. "I'm so sorry. Your first venture into selflessness and you get smacked in the face with a . . . curse."

"Yes," he said haughtily. "But of course, your genuine contrition at having caused my downfall makes up for a lot."

Maggie struggled to straighten her face and said, "I promise I won't force you into any more good deeds."

"I'll bet," he said doubtfully, then smiled reluctantly as she began to laugh again. "Come on, trouble, or we'll miss the boat."

Instead of finding the sailboat waiting for them that Mark had hired the day before, Maggie was surprised to find Mark had decided to take out their host's cabin cruiser—which had been furnished with supplies for the day. Today they were completely alone. No friendly crewmen to show them the sights. Just Maggie and Mark and a brilliant blue sky.

Mark insisted on keeping their destination a secret until they anchored in a tiny cove on one of the many uninhabited islets that surrounded the main island. He carried her ashore, calling out to imaginary pirate cronies to come and admire his booty, then returned to the boat for their supplies while Maggie looked around.

It was paradise, a tiny heaven on earth that seemed to whisper the secrets of love and life to anyone who would take the time to listen. And today Maggie was taking the time. Tomorrow would come soon enough, bringing dull things like responsibility and sanity. Today Maggie would grab her bit of paradise and savor every minute.

"Well, how do you like it?" Mark asked from close behind her, his arms reaching around her to pull her back against him.

Turning in his arms, she took a deep breath, inhaling an exotic mixture of Mark, the perfume of the yellow genip flowers, and the salty tang of the ocean. "It's wonderful. A place out of time. It makes me feel we could stay here for years yet on our return find that only hours had passed."

"You want to try it?"

"I'd love to," she said, laughing. "But while I wouldn't be missed, I have a sneaking suspicion that your diligent Mr. Lowe would find us all too soon."

"I suppose you're right." He sighed regretfully. "But it was a lovely thought." His voice sounded strangely wistful, and there was a faraway look in his eyes. Then he looked down at her and smiled. "So we have to make the most of the time we have. Are you ready for a swim?"

"But I didn't bring a suit."

"Oh, dear," he said, grinning slyly. "Did I forget to tell you we would be swimming?"

"You," she said, shaking her head, the gold tips of her hair glinting in the sun as she tapped him on the chest with one accusing finger, "are totally wicked."

"Yes," he agreed complacently. "Now, come on. We're wasting time."

Their hours on the tiny island were enchanted ones. A lovely, shining gift from the gods. They were carried back to a freer, more innocent time when clothing was an unnecessary encumbrance. They laughed and played like children, absorbing the sun and the sea and the beautiful silence.

Mark insisted that Maggie relate the entire story of her life, beginning with the day she was born, and, though she was unable to start quite that early in her life, she did her best to fill him in without boring him too much.

She told him about her loving but strict parents and about her two younger sisters, who had always seemed to be Maggie's special responsibility. It seemed that she had been pulling them out of scrapes for as long as she could remember. They still called occasionally with a frantic request for aid, and Maggie always gave in to their pleas.

"So that's why you take life so seriously," he

murmured thoughtfully as he sat under a coconut tree, leaning back against a large rock. "You had adult responsibilities even when you were a child."

"Do you think I'm too serious?" she asked, frowning.

"I didn't mean it like that, Maggie," he said. "You have a wonderful—if occasionally sadistic— sense of humor."

"Sadistic?"

"Well, it certainly seems sadistic when you're laughing at me," he said ruefully.

"Would I laugh at you?" she asked innocently, raising up on her knees and leaning across to tweak the hair on his chest.

"Yes, you little demon, you would. And now that I know all about your past, why don't you tell me about your future?"

"Aren't you sick of listening to me? Why don't you tell me about your childhood? I'll bet you were an—" she paused, glancing up at him impishly, "interesting child."

"I'll have you know I was a perfect child. Just as I'm now a perfect adult."

"Perfect?" she scoffed.

"Almost perfect," he said, falling suddenly to the blanket and pulling her with him. "I have one small fault."

"Only one? And what's that?"

He began running one long finger down her throat and across one firm, round breast, then whispered softly in her ear, "I have no patience at all, princess. And I've waited long enough for one day." He then began to make their perfect day complete.

* * *

As they lay on their blanket in the sand, replete with food and love, Maggie saw in one terrible flash what waited for them tomorrow, and she wanted to hold on to the magic for a little longer. She knew this was fantasy and would end when reality forced its way upon them, but for one brief moment she wanted to turn her back on the real world and give herself up to the dream.

"What are you thinking about?" Mark murmured in her ear.

"Oh, dull things like tomorrow." She turned over on her side and ran her hand over his chest, ruffling the fine hair. Stubbornly, Maggie pushed away the picture of the future and replaced it with one that would stick in her mind forever. A picture of Mark standing knee-deep in the ocean, his face raised to the sun, his blond hair darkened to gold by the water.

"Dallas isn't exactly St. Thomas," he said quietly, "but no place is dull if you're with the right person." He turned his head to face her. "Maggie, about tomorrow . . ."

Maggie tugged playfully at the short curly hair. "I don't want to think about tomorrow or Dallas," she said, grinning mischievously. "I want to think about a handsome blond beachcomber and a tiny turquoise cove."

"I love the life of a beachcomber," he said, pulling her over so that she lay on top of him, molding and smoothing her buttocks as though they fascinated him. "You find such interesting things that have washed ashore." Threading his fingers through her hair to pull her head to his chest, he sighed against her forehead and said, "I'm afraid it's time to leave paradise, love."

Then suddenly he framed her face with his

hands, holding her head so that he could look into her eyes, his own turning a deep, steel gray and containing something that looked almost like fear. "Let's stay, Maggie," he whispered urgently. "Let's never go back."

For the moment she was caught up in the unknown vision that held Mark in its grip; then she shook it off to scramble to her feet. "We can't stay, silly. Where would I buy nail polish?"

"The ever-cautious Maggie," he murmured softly, his eyes closed, then rose slowly to his feet. "Okay, woman," he said, slapping her on the rear, "let's stow this gear."

That night Mark had the nightmare again. He woke Maggie with his muffled cries, his face drenched in perspiration, a look of anguish twisting the strong lines of his face. And again Maggie held and soothed him, responding to his terrible urgency with a desperation of her own. The night before had been a leisurely, magical pleasuring. Tonight was raw need—a primitive, hungry mating. They came together in a wild, passionate coupling that touched the hidden depths in each of them, bringing them to a soul-shaking culmination that rocked their little piece of earth. And there was no peaceful sleep for them afterward. They lay holding each other, making love again and again, as though they were storing the loving away to hold them through harder, leaner times.

The next morning Maggie tried to act as though it were just another day, as though it weren't the end of a beautiful dream. But Mark was silent, watching her closely as she packed, and throughout the long trip back to Dallas, a look of reluctant resignation grew in his eyes.

They were met at the airport by the same attractive young man, but this time Maggie made no attempt to respond to his smiling enthusiasm. She looked around her at all the signs of civilization and realized that the invisible labels that separated her world from Mark's were already beginning to show. She carefully avoided his eyes as she slowly let go of the fantasy that had held her in its grip for days.

On their arrival at her apartment, when the bags had been transferred to her strangely foreign living room and the young man had returned to the car to wait, Maggie turned finally to meet Mark's eyes.

"That's it, then, isn't it?" he asked quietly. "You've had your frivolous fling and now it's back to normal, with no room in your orderly life for a court jester."

"Mark," she began, struck for the first time by the uncomfortable feeling that she had used him thoughtlessly, "I—"

"There's no need for explanations, Maggie. I'm not accusing you of anything. You made it very clear why you came with me." Reaching out, he gently smoothed the curls from her forehead with one long finger. "I suppose I hoped you would come to feel differently about it." Leaning down, he touched his lips to her brow, giving her a tender, lingering kiss. "Goodbye, love."

As he walked away she saw him once again, standing knee-deep in the ocean, his face lifted to the sun. She smiled a small, wistful smile, then murmured softly, her voice shaking unexplainably, "Goodbye, Mark."

Chapter Eight

He was there again.

Maggie could see him leaning against a lamp-post across the street, nodding affably to the passers-by, pretending he wasn't following her. All week long she had seen him. Every time she left the office he was there, somewhere in the crowds that lined the downtown streets.

At first she had thought she was mistaken, that it was not him at all, but only someone who looked like him. But when she caught a glimpse of his silver eyes, a new thought took hold. Perhaps her week of ceaselessly dreaming of him had conjured his lean figure to pacify her fevered brain.

Then, exactly one week after they had said goodbye, she was looking into the display window of a department store and there he was, standing behind her, carefully studying a garish brass unicorn.

Turning to the two plump shoppers standing beside him, he said, "Yes, I agree, ladies. He is well worth the money. But then, of course, I'm only a man. What we need is a woman's opinion. I'm sure my wife will be glad to help." He turned to Maggie then, his gray eyes sparkling with fun. "Don't you think he's lovely, dear?"

"I think he's totally unprincipled," she whispered before walking briskly away from him, feeling the curious stares of the duo beside Mark. As she walked her face was completely composed, but her heart, her unruly heart, was bursting with unexplainable joy.

Mark didn't come after her that day, but in the week that followed she saw his blond head above the crowd, felt his eyes following every step she took. He was there when she went to lunch and when she walked to her car every evening. And when she and Carrel joined hundreds of other lunchtime shoppers in bargain hunting—he was there.

Maggie didn't try to hide from Mark. She simply did her best to ignore him. But of course, that was easier said than done. Mark was certainly not the easiest man in the world to ignore. And Carrel didn't help matters at all. Several times Maggie caught her waving to him when she thought Maggie wasn't looking.

Maggie had tried, without success, to convince Carrel that she was handling things in the only way she knew how. One evening as they shared a pizza in front of Maggie's television, Carrel again brought up the subject that was constantly in Maggie's thoughts.

"Explain it to me again," Carrel said as she reached for another piece of pizza. "Explain why you ignore a man who is handsome and charming and rich and—judging by the gleam in your eyes when you look at him—fantastic in bed. All that and crazy about you, too. Tell me again, and maybe this time I'll understand."

Maggie stood and began to pace around the room. Then she stopped and turned to look at her friend. "Don't you remember the discussion we had before I went away with Mark? You said you could see how any kind of relationship between us would be a disaster. Remember?"

"I may have said something like that," Carrel hedged.

"You said exactly that," Maggie said. "Then you decided that a fling would be just the thing I needed. Well, I've had my fling and now it's over."

"Why are you so defensive about it?" Carrel asked calmly. "And don't tell me that you went with Mark because I told you to. I refuse to believe that when he made love to you, you gritted your teeth and pretended he was castor oil."

"Of course I didn't." Maggie sighed. "I went because I wanted to and I enjoyed—" Maggie stopped as the inadequacy of the word struck her. "I loved every minute of it," she amended. "It was beautiful, but I can't relate it to my real life. I can't relate Mark to my real life."

"That's what you keep saying. How do you know you can't? You haven't given him a fair chance."

"A chance to what?" Maggie asked, beginning to pace the floor again. "Be reasonable. Can you really see Mark unobtrusively slipping into the kind of life I live? Can you see him sitting here eating pizza off a paper towel and watching a bowling tournament on television?"

"It's baseball, but I see what you mean. And no, I guess I can't imagine him here."

"Okay, then, can you see me slipping comfortably into Mark's way of life?"

"You could," Carrel insisted, turning sideways on the couch to watch Maggie's pacing. "You could if you wanted to."

"And that's the key," Maggie said. "If I wanted to. I like Mark. I like him a lot, but I don't want to change my life for him. And I would have to if I continued seeing him. Or at least, one of us would have to." She paused, her voice becoming calmer as she continued. "I won't rush into anything again. It makes me uncomfortable, as though I weren't in control of my own life any more. I like to think things over, look beneath the surface, and see how I'll be affected by any particular action in the future."

She stopped pacing and turned to face Carrel. "And there is no future of any kind for Mark and me."

Carrel shook her head sorrowfully. "You're thinking like a computer again, Maggie. I thought you were going to work on that."

"I can't help the way I think. It's part of me. I've got a brain and I've got to use it."

"But can't you see how much you're missing? You say acting impulsively makes you uncomfortable, but wasn't your trip with Mark worth a little discomfort?"

Maggie couldn't answer Carrel's question for a moment. She had to stop and think. Wasn't her time with Mark worth anything? Would she trade what they had shared, those wonderful, magical days, for logic? Maggie didn't have to give much thought to the question. She wouldn't give up her memories for anything.

"It was worth it," she admitted softly, then shook her head as though that would rid her of the confusion. "But it was only a dream. It only existed there. You can't bring dreams home with you in a suitcase, like a seashell. They dissolve when they're exposed to the air in the normal world."

Carrel didn't speak for a moment, and her eyes narrowed thoughtfully as she looked at Maggie. Then she murmured, "I wish I could figure out why you're trying so hard to convince yourself that this thing with Mark wouldn't work."

Maggie sighed in exasperation. "I'm not making this up, Carrel. These are facts. Indisputable facts."

"But what about feelings? You're getting so hung up on those damn facts that you're forgetting about emotions. You haven't said a word about how you feel."

"I feel like I'm being tracked by a bloodhound," Maggie said, smiling wryly. 'Now are you satisfied?"

"I don't think you've given yourself a chance to think about how you feel," Carrel said. "Why is that? You always examine everything so carefully. Why haven't you taken your emotions out and examined them, too? Is there something you're afraid of, Maggie?"

Maggie couldn't stand any more. She felt as though her brain were being pulled in a dozen different directions. She walked around to sit beside Carrel and said quietly, "I can't think about it any more tonight. Would you just take my word for it? I know it's wrong, and that's why I'm pretending he's not there."

Carrel did not want to accept Maggie's evasion,

but she knew her friend well enough to drop the subject—for the time being. After that night she resorted to subtle hints and gentle reminders that effectively kept Mark in Maggie's mind—even when she could not see him—yet didn't force her into a confrontation of her feelings for him.

"Maggie," Carrel said one day, picking up the banner again as she casually glanced at Mark who was looking through the merchandise on a sale table. "I think you should at least give him "E" for effort. He certainly doesn't give up."

"He warned me once that he doesn't handle defeat well," Maggie explained wearily, tiring suddenly of fighting herself as well as Carrel and Mark. "I'm the one who got away." They moved along then to another table, with Mark close behind. "You know how the mind can blow things like this out of proportion," she added, trying to convince herself. "It's the chance that you missed that always afterward seems like the golden opportunity."

"Maybe," Carrel replied doubtfully. "But I still think there's more to him than meets the eye."

And of course there was. Maggie knew very well that Mark had hidden depths, but she also knew that she could not continue seeing him without being hurt. That much she would admit to herself. If they picked up the affair where they had left off, Mark would absorb her completely. She would not be able to keep him separate from what she considered her real life. And if the affair went a step further, into a more permanent relationship, deep down Maggie was afraid she would come to feel the contempt she had secretly held for Barry. She couldn't risk losing the beautiful dream they had shared on St. Thomas for a less-than-beautiful reality.

So she continued to ignore Mark, pretending she didn't see him following her, just as she was pretending now that she didn't see him crossing the street and walking toward her. She quickly turned down the little side street where her car was parked, walking faster when she heard footsteps close behind her. She was only a few feet away from her car when she felt his hand on her arm, pulling her to a halt, turning her to face him.

"Hello, Maggie Simms," he said softly, looking into her eyes with a hesitant, slightly crooked smile.

The hesitancy, the uncertainty of his touch, broke her. All her carefully formulated objections flew right out of her head. She couldn't have remained aloof with a will one hundred times as strong. "Oh, Mark," she whispered, her lower lip quivering uncontrollably as he hauled her into his arms, holding her fiercely, oblivious to the stares of the passing world.

Chapter Nine

In the weeks that followed, Maggie saw not one trace of the uncertainty that Mark had shown when he had confronted her. He teased and laughed and gave ridiculous excuses for having pursued her so persistently, but the hint of vulnerability was gone, leading her to believe that it was just one of the many guises he could pull at will from his enormous repertoire.

But it didn't matter. His vulnerability—assumed or not—had merely served as a catalyst that brought her own to the surface. She wanted to be with him. It was as simple as that. However mismatched they were, she wanted him. So she had called on the age-old trick of ignoring the unpleasant facts in favor of those she wished to see. While she knew that eventually things would come to a head, she decided to take things as they came and handle the problems if and when they surfaced.

Carefully closing her mind to the nagging voice of her Calvinist background, she gave herself up to the deep, abiding pleasure of Mark's presence. She let the tide of laughter and sensual feeling wash over her and carry her away from her logical, orderly world.

Three weeks later, as they drove through the quiet countryside on their way to see Jake, Maggie faced the fact that soon she would have to deal with problem number one. Although she was with Mark physically every night and mentally all through her working day, she could see that this arrangement was rapidly becoming inadequate for their needs. Mark was already spending more time in her home than he was his own. And it was getting more and more difficult for them to say good night at the end of each evening when he went home.

So what did she do? Suggest that he move into her tiny apartment? Or should she give up the home she had made for herself to move in with him until the affair ended? Mark was being very careful not to tread on the sensitive toes of her independence, but she knew that the situation was harder on him than it was on her. He was the one who had to leave each evening.

She looked around to find that they had turned off on the narrow oiled road that led to the lodge, and Maggie shelved the problem with a mental promise to attack it at the first opportunity.

"You've been awfully quiet," Mark said as they pulled into the small gravel parking lot. "Is something wrong?"

"I'm just enjoying the quiet. It's been a hectic week."

He watched her closely as they walked to the

large wooden door, then said quietly, "Just say the word, Maggie, and we'll fly away to a place where they've never even heard of a sales consultant."

"Don't tempt me." She laughed, then turned to greet Jake as he opened the door for them.

She had seen Jake on many occasions in the past, but now, knowing he had helped to make Mark the man he was, she looked at him with new eyes. How could this rough, homey man have been even partially responsible for the suave Mark? Whatever Jake had given him must be beneath the surface, hidden from the naked eye.

Jake welcomed them warmly into the large, open room that looked out over the small, twenty-acre lake. He had no guests, for the room was empty and no boats were visible on the lake.

After Mark had seated himself beside Maggie on the long, low sofa, he said, "Well, old man, what's this I hear about your falling in the lake again?"

"Again?" Jake asked gruffly. "You're gonna give Maggie, here, the idea that I make a habit of tryin' to drown myself."

"Well, don't you?" Mark asked, grinning widely. "I seem to remember a time a few years back when you took a nose dive off the dock into shallow water and came up spitting mud and curses a mule skinner would have been proud to use."

Jake shook his head sadly, his pale eyes twinkling with merriment. "You've got the devil in you for sure, boy. You had it then, and I sure don't see any signs of its dissipating."

"Surely you don't blame me," Mark said in mock surprise, then turned to Maggie to explain. "I was twelve years old at the time and I had just caught the granddaddy bass of all time. I would have landed him just fine if Jake hadn't gotten so excited that he tripped over his own legs and fell in the lake."

"For shame, Mark," Jake reprimanded. "Filling Maggie's head full of lies like that. Don't listen to him, darlin'. That long-legged limb of satan stuck out his foot on purpose just to see me take a dip."

"A vicious canard," Mark replied sadly. "Nothing but a vicious canard."

"Oh, talk English for once," Jake muttered. "And if that means the God Almighty truth, then I agree."

Maggie laughed along with the two men, enjoying their good-natured banter. The argument was apparently an old one, for soon the insults were coming fast and furious, each one more outrageous than the last.

Mark finally ended it by saying, "I don't care what you say: the truth is, you caused me to lose a record bass. Now, tell me, who threw you in the lake this time?"

"It's that damned dock. It should have been replaced years ago," Jake said, rubbing his weathered jaw. "I was leaning down to check one of the posts and lost my balance."

"Was the post rotted out like you thought?"

"Yeah, there's three of 'em that need replacing," he replied. "I'll get Harv and Shorty on it next week."

Mark stood. "Why don't I have a look at them while I'm here?"

"Now, sit down, son. There's no need for you to do that. The men will get to it when they have time."

"I want to, Jake." He turned to smile at Maggie. "You don't mind if I leave you with this old reprobate, do you?"

"Of course I don't mind," Maggie said over Jake's indignant snort. "Jake and I can compare notes about a certain self-satisfied man we both know."

"That sounds vaguely ominous." Mark laughed. "Perhaps I should stay to protect my image."

"Oh, go on, boy. Git," Jake said, shooing Mark away. "Me and Maggie are going to have a nice talk. If your image is just one-half as good as you think it is, it'll hold up."

As Mark left the room chuckling, Jake turned to Maggie. "Now tell me what that scoundrel's been up to, Maggie. I can't tell you how tickled I was when he told me you two had gotten together."

"Thank you," Maggie murmured. "I still find it hard to believe he's your nephew."

"So do I sometimes," the old man muttered, more to himself than to Maggie. "He used to practically live with me and Jennie. You never met Jennie, did you, Maggie?" He smiled slowly, his eyes taking on a soft, reminiscent quality. "She was the most beautiful thing God ever put on this earth. And she thought the sun rose and set in Mark's eyes. When we found out we'd never have kids, I thought her heart would break in pure sorrow. Then Mark came along. His mama was sickly, and Jonathan—Jon's my brother—he never seemed to have time for the boy. So me and Jennie got him every summer. That is, 'til old Marcus decided he was old enough to start learning all about big business."

He sighed heavily, a tired sound. "I sure hated to see him stop coming—mainly for Jennie's sake and because I loved him myself, but partly because I knew what my father and his circus of fools could do to a person. He tried the same thing on me fifty years ago."

"He wanted you to take over?" Maggie asked, finding it hard to imagine this man, with his stooped frame and his gnarled, work-roughened hands, in Mark's world.

"He sure did. He knew Jonathan would never have a head for business, so I was his only other choice. When I saw which way the wind was blowing, I lit out. I roamed around the country for a couple of years, picking fruit and washing dishes. Then I discovered East Texas and my Jennie." A light shone deep in the old man's faded gray eyes, and for a moment they looked remarkably like Mark's. "I knew the minute I saw her that she was what I was looking for—and I didn't even know I was looking. She was the little, bittiest thing you ever saw. And she was true clear through to the middle. I gotta tell you, Maggie, for a while I was tempted to go back and take old Marcus up on his offer, just so I could give Jennie the fine things she deserved. But she knew. Yessir, my Jennie knew what I was thinking, and she turned as stubborn as an old mule. She said she wasn't cut out to be high society and all she wanted was me and a house full of my kids. So I bought this place from Dan Kingman for her. God didn't see fit to give us those kids, but he made it up to us by sending Mark. If I didn't love Mark for himself, I'd love him for the happiness I saw in Jennie's eyes when she looked at him."

He sighed and seemed to draw himself back to the present. "I don't think I've said so many words in one sitting in twenty years. I didn't know I still had that much wind left in me. You're a good listener, Maggie." He reached across from his chair and patted her hand. "Now tell me what you think of my boy."

"That's a tall order, Jake," she said, shaking her head ruefully. "I've asked myself the same question dozens of times. Sometimes—usually, in fact—I think I don't know him well enough to have an opinion. I just know I love being with him."

"That's enough for now. The rest will take care of itself. Now let's go see if our supper is about ready."

After they had stood for a while in the kitchen talking to his large, cheerful housekeeper, Jake sent Maggie out to tell Mark that dinner was almost ready. She walked slowly in the direction of the dock, thinking about her conversation with Mark's uncle. All through their talk she had had the strangest feeling that he was trying to tell her something. Jake was not a man to give unasked-for advice. He had been making a statement of some kind and was evidently leaving her to figure it out on her own.

As she neared the dock a splash drew her thoughts away from the puzzling conversation, and she focused on a figure standing on the far side of the dock. It looked like . . . no, it couldn't possibly be Mark.

"Mark!" she gasped as she drew near enough to confirm her suspicion. "My Lord, you're covered with . . . mud!"

He looked up from the post he was pulling loose, to see her standing on the bank, then looked down at his bare, mud-smeared chest. "Why, yes. So I am," he replied, giving the post one last hard yank, then walking to lay it on the bank. "But on me even mud takes on a new elegance, don't you think?"

"You're impossible," she said, backing away as he threatened to· hug her. "How are you going to sit down to dinner?"

"I keep a few clothes here. Now, stop backing away from me. Haven't you ever made love in the mud?"

"No. And I'm not about to start now. I still can't believe you're actually out here playing in the mud. I've never seen you mussed before."

"If I can't carry off a little mud with dignity and style, then I've lost my touch," he said haughtily, then laughed as she continued to stare in astonishment. "Come on, love. We'd better get back before Jake sends out a search party. I presume he sent you to fetch me."

"Yes. Dinner's almost ready," she said, walking beside him but carefully avoiding bumping into him.

"So what did you and Jake talk about? Did he let you in on the secrets of my past?"

"A few."

"And did you let him in on the secrets of my present?"

She smiled, thinking again how little she really knew about Mark. "I'm afraid your present secrets are still secrets, because I haven't a clue. I'm simply riding in your wake."

He stopped walking to look down at her. "Is that the way you see it?" He smiled a strange little smile. "How odd," he murmured, then began to walk again, changing the subject before she could comment. "How do you think Jake looks? I've been worried about him lately. The last time I was here—on the memorable weekend that we met—he was recovering from a bout with pneumonia."

"He seems fine to me. I've never known him to talk so much. He told me about your Aunt Jennie."

"Did he? We don't usually talk about her. It's

been twenty years since she died, but we both still miss her."

"She must have been a very special person," Maggie said. Mark's voice held the same quiet sadness that Jake's had when he had spoken of his Jennie, and Maggie wondered what kind of woman could have made such an impression on these two strong men.

"She was the best," he said simply.

They entered by the back way to avoid tracking mud into the living room, and Maggie stayed to talk with Jake about Maggie's aunt and uncle, while Mark went to shower. Later they joined Mark in the living room to wait on the last-minute preparations for dinner.

Mark sat on the sofa, pulling Maggie down beside him after mixing them both what he termed the perfect après-mud drink. Jake reclaimed his former position, watching them with a peculiar look in his eyes.

All through dinner he rarely took his eyes off Maggie and Mark, listening closely to their light-hearted teasing, and he seemed to grow more uneasy as the night wore on.

When they were preparing to leave, Jake took Maggie aside, out of range of Mark's hearing. "Maggie," he said hesitantly, "sometime soon do you think you could come back to see me . . . alone?"

"Of course, Jake," she said, puzzled by his request. "Was there anything in particular you wanted to discuss with me?"

He started to reply, but when he saw Mark moving in their direction, he seemed to change his mind and said jokingly, "Oh, just this and that and the price of shoes, darlin'. Now, you better go. Mark'll get jealous seeing you whispering secrets with a fine-lookin' man like me."

"I heard that, you old derelict. Trying to steal my woman, are you?" Mark asked, grinning.

"All's fair, boy. All's fair."

Jake stood in the door, waving as they drove away. Maggie turned around in her seat to give one last wave, then leaned back with a sigh, saying, "He's a wonderful old man. So warm and natural. You were lucky to have him and Jennie."

"Although I agree with you, love, I think I'm also a little jealous. I'm the only man you're supposed to find wonderful." He pulled the car over to the side of the road. "Do you see where we are?"

Maggie looked around. They were parked in front of her aunt and uncle's house, which lay in darkness. "Yes, but why are we stopping? Aunt Sarah and Uncle Charles always go to bed with the sun."

Leaning over, Mark put his arm around her and whispered in her ear, "There's a mound of dirt behind that house"—he nipped her earlobe gently—"that covers a cozy little cave"—he moved to kiss the sensitive skin behind her ear—"which holds some very lovely and some very frustrating memories. If I weren't afraid your uncle would shoot us as prowlers, I would carry you into that cavern and finish what we started there."

Excitement shot through her veins, singing dizzily in her ears. She turned her head, touching his neck softly with her lips. "I wouldn't want you to feel cheated," she murmured huskily. "We could always turn off all the lights in my apartment and sleep on the floor."

"Once I get you alone in your apartment, I doubt we'll get past the living-room floor," he said, his breath hot on her lips as his head descended. "I could eat you up right now." He traced the line of her lips with his warm, moist tongue before plunging it into the sweet depths of her mouth. Maggie met his tongue hungrily as the urgency built in each of them.

"My God, princess," he groaned, clasping her head to his chest. "What am I going to do with you?"

Maggie snaked her hand around his waist, feeling the warmth beneath his clothes. "I could make a few suggestions," she whispered shakily.

Giving a broken laugh, he released her slowly. "We had better leave now, before we risk shocking your relatives."

The drive back to Dallas seemed to take years, and when they finally arrived at Maggie's apartment, she found Mark's prediction to be accurate. They made it no farther than the furry living-room rug before giving in to the passion that raged in them both.

"Maggie, for heaven's sake, what are you doing?" Mark asked as he stood waiting for her to catch up with him. "Our reservation was for eight and it's eight-fifteen now."

She looked up belligerently as she walked to stand beside him. "And whose fault is that? I was ready to go. You're the one who had to watch the rest of that dumb situation comedy."

"It wasn't dumb," he protested, taking her arm as they walked. "It was a sensitive portrayal of the problems encountered by a transvestite hockey player."

"You idiot." She laughed. "It was about an advertising executive and his wife."

"Oh, was that his wife? I suppose it was the mustache that threw me off."

Maggie's laughter was interrupted by increasingly loud shouts from across the parking lot. The vulgarisms seemed out of place in the beautifully landscaped grounds of the Greek restaurant where they were about to dine. Maggie leaned around Mark to find out what was going on and saw three men standing under a tree, their angry curses attracting the attention of several people leaving the restaurant.

"Mark, they're bullying him," she gasped.

Mark tightened his hold on her arm and continued walking toward the entrance. "Stay out of it, Maggie," he said firmly.

"But he's just a boy."

He stopped abruptly, turning her to look at him. "Maggie, you cannot butt into other people's personal business." He gave her a little shake. "Now, no one is being hurt. They're simply arguing."

"But he's so young, and I saw one of them shove him." She looked up, her eyes pleading. "Couldn't you just check to make sure he doesn't need help?"

"You promised you wouldn't get me into this kind of thing again," he reminded her, then looked into her eyes and sighed in resignation. "Okay, okay. But you stay right here."

She watched in tense silence as he walked toward the trio. They turned as Mark approached, eyeing him curiously. From where she stood, Maggie couldn't hear what was being said, but she could tell the three men were listening closely to what Mark was saying. Then suddenly all she could see were flying fists and she ran toward them, shouting as she went. When she arrived, out of breath, the trio was walking away and Mark was leaning against the tree, holding his handkerchief to his eyes.

"Mark?" she said hesitantly. "Are you all right?"

Slowly he lowered the handkerchief, exposing some angry-looking scratches and a red and puffy eye which promised to be the most vivid shiner she had ever seen. He looked at Maggie, his eyes blazing, and spoke through clenched teeth. "If you ever . . . so much as look like you're about to volunteer my help again, so help me, Maggie, I'll hold you up by your toes until that busy little nose of yours turns blue."

"I promise," she said, torn between laughter and tears. "Never. Never again." She reached up to touch his face. "I'm so sorry, Mark. I seem to make a habit of saying that, don't I? Does it hurt much? It looks"—she swallowed a semihysterical giggle—"awful."

He looked suspiciously at her sober face, then said irritably, "I'm not exactly fond of pain, but no, it's not bad. And you can stop squelching that laugh. I can't hear it, but I can definitely see it in your eyes."

"No, you're wrong," she protested. "At least, I'm not amused by your pain. It's just . . ." She paused and looked again at the crimson and swelling skin that she had been carefully avoiding. "It looks so strange." His eyes told her immediately that she had said the wrong thing. He looked at her as if she were a pesky fly that had irritated him once too often, so she said hurriedly, "Why don't we go home so I can put an ice pack on it? I can fix you something to eat and . . ." She stopped as something besides irritation began to form in his eyes.

"And what, Maggie?"

"And . . . oh, I don't know. I guess I can apologize for getting you into a scrape and try to make up for it."

"And just how do you propose to do that?" he said, making no effort to hide his growing amusement.

"Well, certainly not the way you think," she fumed. "And if you're not going to be gracious enough to accept my apology, then you can just forget the whole thing."

"But I always accept everything you offer me graciously, love. And if you truly want to make up for being the cause of my excruciating pain, I'm sure we can work something out." He was laughing openly now.

"You are the most—" she began, her eyes blazing.

"Adorable, intelligent, handsome, *forgiving* man you've ever met," he finished for her. "That is what you were going to say, isn't it?"

Maggie looked into his eyes, ready to blast him, when suddenly her anger died. It was impossible to stay mad at him. He was so damn cute. "Yes," she murmured. "Now that you mention it, I guess that is what I was going to say."

For a moment he looked as though her answer had taken him by surprise, then slowly he began to smile and together they walked back across the parking lot to his car.

Back at Maggie's apartment, Mark consumed an enormous cheese omelet, then lay on the sofa, his head in her lap so she could apply the ice pack and a soothing hand to his brow.

Looking up at her with one gleaming silver eye, he asked, "Did you see which of the malodorous cretins dropped the Brooklyn Bridge on my face?"

"Well, actually . . ." She hesitated, avoiding his eye.

"Which one, Maggie?" he demanded.

"It was the boy," she admitted with a sigh.

"That pimple-faced little cur?" he shouted, pulling off the ice pack to stare in surprise. "But he couldn't have weighed more than a hundred and twenty pounds."

"He sneaked the punch in when you weren't looking," she soothed. "And anyway, I think you broke the fat one's nose."

"Did I?" He looked somewhat mollified by the information, replacing the ice pack with a sigh.

"Mark, why did they start punching? What on earth did you say?"

"I simply asked them politely to move their quarrel to a less public location, but they made it quite clear that they resented my interference." He removed the ice pack again to look at her. "Maggie," he said quietly. "I'm not Sir Lancelot. Not now, not ever. I would fight the city of Dallas en masse to keep you or Jake from being hurt, but I can't play Don Quixote even for you."

"I don't expect—" she began.

"But you do, love," he said, sitting up and pulling her into his arms. "Maybe not consciously, but somewhere inside you, you expect me to be something I'm not and never could be." He tilted her chin with his fingers. "Couldn't you possibly accept me as I am?"

Maggie laughed uncertainly, looking away from his observant eyes. "Don't be silly. Why should I not accept you the way you are?"

"Ah, love." He sighed heavily, closing his eyes as though disappointed in her answer. Then he opened them to murmur, "What happened to your plans to make it up to me for causing me to become entangled in a common brawl?"

Maggie smiled and slowly began unbuttoning his shirt, loving the feel of him, unaccountably relieved that the discussion had been postponed. She spread his shirt wide, running her hands across his chest, wondering if their lovemaking would ever be ordinary and mechanical. They had been together for over a month and still came together each time with a renewed hunger. Each time was new and wondrous and so right. And as long as this was right, all the rest seemed to fade into the background for Maggie.

She leaned her head forward, her tongue beginning to tease the stiff male nipples that her fingers had discovered. But Mark, breaking under the erotic torture with a deep growl, grasped her head suddenly between his hands, pulling her up to meet his lips—and the magic began again.

Maggie woke the next morning in Mark's arms, immeasurably glad she had asked him to spend the night. The warmth of having him beside her reached more than her flesh. She felt it all the way through her body. If she could only bottle the feeling, she felt she could cure the ills of the world.

Stretching lazily she caught sight of the clock on the nightstand. "Oh, Lord," she moaned. It was six-thirty already. If she didn't move quickly, she would be late for work. She turned to slip from the bed, but felt a large, warm hand snake around her bare waist to detain her.

"Deserting one's post is a serious offense," he murmured huskily, moving to half-cover her body.

"I know," she whispered regretfully. "But time

and Howard Electronics wait for no man. It's Monday and I have to go make peanut butter money."

Smoothing the curls from her forehead with a gentle, lingering touch, he said, as though the idea had just hit him, "Maggie, why don't you quit? No, wait and let me finish. We could get married. Then you wouldn't have to work and I wouldn't have to go home to an empty bed each night."

Maggie felt a whirling rush of warmth spread through her veins. She hadn't anticipated his proposal, and she certainly hadn't anticipated her reaction to it. What was wrong with her? Before she could gather her chaotic thoughts enough to form a reply of any kind, he continued.

"It would be such fun, love. We could go where we please and do what we want."

Fun? she thought, her heated blood cooling with the word, a shaft of deep, unexplainable pain striking her dead center. But of course he wanted fun. What had she expected, undying love? She closed her eyes against the thought, taking a deep breath to gain control, then opened them to find him watching her. "You're a nut," she laughed shakily. "People don't get married to have fun. At least, sensible people don't."

She slid from his grasp and walked to the closet to remove her robe. As she pulled it on she said, "I know this arrangement hasn't been too convenient for either of us, but we can work something out. Something a little less drastic than marriage."

As she walked into the bathroom for her shower, Mark lay where she had left him, silently examining the ceiling, but by the time she had finished showering and dressing, the carefree manner had reappeared, and before she left for work, he had arranged to pick her up for dinner as usual.

Maggie wished it were as easy for her to return to normal. Confusing thoughts pounded away at her head and by lunchtime had taken their toll, leaving her with a blinding headache. She sat in a little sandwich shop with Carrel, toying with her sandwich until Carrel could stand her lassitude no longer.

"Maggie," she said, the exasperation in her voice making Maggie flinch in pain. "What on earth is wrong with you? You've been a zombie all day. It's positively eerie."

"Mark proposed," Maggie replied dully.

"But that's wonderful!" Carrel said enthusiastically. "Why are you acting like the bottom just dropped out of the market?"

"It's not wonderful. It's—"

"Yes. It is," Carrel insisted. "I've been so worried about you. I could see how much you loved him and I was afraid you'd be hurt, but if you're going to marry him—"

"Love?" Maggie asked, shock widening her eyes. "I don't . . ." She stopped as the truth hit her with a sharp pain. "Oh, God," she moaned. "Of course, I love him. How could I be so stupid?"

"Now what's wrong? You love him. He proposed. What could be more perfect?"

"Carrel," Maggie said, the pain in her chest restricting her speech. "He wants to marry me because it will be fun."

"Of course it will be fun," her friend replied in confusion.

"You don't understand," she whispered, biting her lip to control the quivering. "He doesn't love me. He wants me and we have fun together, but he doesn't love me. And I want to be loved, Carey.

I want to be loved by him. The way Jake loved—still loves—Jennie. The way I love Mark."

"Oh, honey," Carrel said, laying her hand on Maggie's. "Don't you think you're asking too much? The kind of love Jake had for Jennie—that's a one in a million thing. Don't you think you should take what you can get? Believe me, it's more than most people get a chance at."

"I just don't know." Maggie sighed. "He didn't even mind when I turned him down."

"So tell him you've reconsidered, marry him, and then work for what you want," Carrel said urgently. "You've got a good start, Maggie. Build on it."

The rest of the day was a total loss as far as Maggie's work was concerned. She couldn't get Mark out of her mind. Build on it, Carrel had said. Build on what? All they had going for them was Maggie's love and an overpowering physical attraction. They were worlds apart in every other way. How could they build on such shifting sand? And would Mark even want to? If it got to be too much of an effort, if it stopped being fun, wouldn't he simply give up? Then where would Maggie be? She'd be out in the cold, much worse off than she was now, because she would have gotten used to loving him, would have built up her hopes so high that she would be completely devastated when it was over.

She couldn't imagine any pain worse than what she was feeling now, but logically she knew that it would be much, much worse later, when she had come to depend on him. And that would be like trying to depend on a butterfly.

No, she had to get out of it now, before the damage was too great. She had to call him and break their date for this evening, then find a way to tell him it was over. It wouldn't be easy, she knew. Mark really cared for her in his own way, and she didn't want to hurt him. But she was fighting for her life now, and she would find the strength somehow.

Picking up the phone, she dialed Mark's office number and asked for Mark when she heard the soft, feminine voice of his secretary.

Mark's voice was warm and low as he asked without greeting her, "How did you know I was thinking of you?"

Maggie swallowed hard and closed her eyes. She had known it would be difficult, but she could never have imagined the pain she felt at simply hearing his voice. "I guess I'm psychic," she said, her voice strained.

"Is something wrong, love?"

"Well, actually there is, Mark." She paused, feeling his tension through the wire. "Something's come up, and I won't be able to see you tonight." The words came in an awkward rush, causing the silence that followed to sound deafening in her ear.

"I see," he said finally. "Well, if it can't be helped, it can't be helped. Shall I call you later this evening?"

"No," she answered quickly, before her nerve failed. "I'll call you tomorrow or"—her throat constricted—"something."

This time the silence drew out until she felt she would scream. Then his voice, stiff and slow, came over the line again. "Very well, Maggie. If that's what you want." Then the phone was dead.

No, she moaned silently, it's not what I want. I want you. I want your love. Maggie took a deep breath, the muscles of her face tightening to keep

the pain from overflowing. She suddenly felt someone watching her and looked up to see Carrel
leaning against the partition wall.

"Why?" Carrel asked.

"He could break me," Maggie whispered through
tight lips. "When he flew away to something that
was more amusing, it would kill me. I know it
would."

Carrel turned away, shaking her head in disgust,
then looked back at her to say quietly, "You're a
coward, Maggie." She picked up her purse and
left without looking back.

And so went the beginning of the end, Maggie
thought as she drove home. If the pain is this bad
when I try to break one date, what is it going to be
like when I try to explain that it's over? And what
can I possibly say that will make any sense at all?
Maybe, she thought desperately, when the time
comes I'll know.

But the time came sooner than she had anticipated. When she walked wearily to her apartment
door, she found Mark there, his hands shoved in his
pockets in an uncharacteristically awkward pose.
She stopped short the minute she saw him, then
covered the remaining distance slowly. "Hello," she
said hesitantly. "I didn't expect to see you tonight."

He made no comment, but waited silently for
her to open the door, then followed her into the
living room. His face held a look Maggie had never
seen there before. He looked older, harder. Maggie
glanced away, searching for something to say. She
looked back at him, and the words she had been
forming died in her throat as she met his eyes.

"Do you want to tell me about it, Maggie?" he
asked, a terrible flatness in his voice taking the
place of the usual animation.

There could be no hedging now. She couldn't stall or try to make light of the situation. She owed him the truth. "I can't see you again," she began slowly, her pride demanding that she look him in the eye, her failing courage urging her to look away. Pride won, and she continued. "I'm getting too involved with you, Mark. More deeply than I ever expected or wanted."

"And that's bad?"

"Not bad," she corrected, "but wrong. Wrong for me and, I believe, wrong for you. Can't you see? We're totally different. Not just on the surface, but underneath, where it counts. I can't live the way you live without its eating away at me. And you've already told me you can't live my kind of life. Work bores you silly, and in time so would I."

He stood there, his silver eyes penetrating her skull, not speaking for interminable minutes. Then he said softly, "So you've got it all figured out, have you?" He turned and walked to the window. "But what if you're wrong, Maggie? Have you even considered the possibility? Suppose our lives could mesh out of bed as well as they do in it. Suppose you've been mistaken in your evaluation of my character and in the depth of my feeling for you."

"Have I?" she asked, almost begging him to confirm it. "Am I wrong, Mark?"

He turned to look at her, his eyes growing perceptibly darker for a moment. Then he sighed, his breath coming from his throat in a rough, raspy sound, and said wearily. "The infallible Maggie wrong? Not likely, love. Not likely."

And before she could move, before she could beg him to stay and give her whatever he had to give, he was gone.

Chapter Ten

This time Mark didn't come back. There was no blond head showing above the downtown crowds. No silver eyes following her movements as she waded drearily through the routine that had seemed so important to her before.

It took Maggie two weeks and three disastrous dates with faceless men to know that she had to do something. She either had to come to grips with the situation as it was or make a move to change it. Mark hadn't been out of her mind for five consecutive minutes in the past two weeks.

She had seen him constantly in her mind, reliving the events of their affair. Mark shaking out the burlap bags to make a bed on the floor of the cellar. Mark holding his hand over his heart, telling her with that ridiculous Southern drawl that he fancied her. Mark standing beside her, his naked body gleaming in the sun.

Oh, God, she moaned silently, her hands covering her face as she sat in her dark living room, fighting a losing battle against the memories of Mark. Then, suddenly, different memories flooded her mind. The look in his eyes when she had told him she wouldn't respect herself if she slept with him. The way he had drawn back, refusing to seduce her when she had had too much to drink. The vulnerability that had shown in his face the day he had confronted her on the street. His concern for Jake. His unfailing tenderness, his gentle understanding.

A terrible heaviness settled on her chest, and she knew then that she was admitting for the first time the things she had always known. Mark was a man to be admired. A man who enjoyed life, and, for her, made it worth living. She had been so caught up in the care-for-nothing facade Mark showed the word that she had ignored the sensitive man underneath. And she had had many glimpses of the sensitive Mark. How could she have been so blind? How could she have not seen the man she had fallen in love with? The sensual Mark had held her body captive. The court jester had captured her imagination. But it was the vulnerable, sensitive Mark who had won and held her heart.

And she had let him go.

No, she hadn't let him go—she had shoved him away. And not for anything so noble as principles. For stupid, crippling pride. Maggie was afraid of failing again. It was that simple. She was afraid she didn't have what it took to hold a man like Mark. So she had given up before the battle even started.

As that realization sank in, the pain became

unbearable. It screamed inside her head and ripped at her chest. She was dying. She was sitting in this dark, quiet, lonely room and she was dying. And she had brought it on herself. Her damned stupidity, her abominable pride, her . . .

"My God," she whispered, standing abruptly and wiping the dampness from her cheeks with trembling hands. "I'm getting maudlin. Why in the hell am I sitting here moaning and feeling oh, so sorry for myself? I've got to *do* something."

She would go to see him, she decided, walking quickly into the bedroom to change. She reached in to pull out a dress, then let her hand fall back to her side. She couldn't confront him, out of the blue, with her feelings. It wouldn't be fair. He would feel obligated to pick up their affair again, and from his silence in the last two weeks it was clear that he had adjusted quickly to being without her.

But Maggie had to let him know the real reason she had sent him away. She had to tell him how she had closed her eyes to his true character. She couldn't let him continue to think that she held a low opinion of him—and Maggie needed to tell him of her love.

Finally deciding a letter was the only way to handle it fairly, she sat down to write. A letter would let him know her feelings yet call for no response on his part. He could throw it in the trash and forget it if he wished.

After three hours of trying to explain on paper, only to crumble each effort in disgust, she finally settled for a simple statement of fact. It read:

Dear Mark,
    This is the most difficult letter I've ever tried to write. I've searched desperately for a way to

excuse my behavior toward you during our association but have found none. You were wrong, Mark. I'm not infallible. In fact I'm probably the most fallible person you could find. I've thought of you constantly for the past two weeks, and one thing has become clear. You're a man such as I've never known before. Maybe that's why I was so slow to open my eyes. I was blind to your sensitivity, your tenderness, and your strength. I was also blind to the fact that I love you.

I hope you can forgive me for running scared from the unknown quantity of my love for you. I know I never will.

Maggie

Maggie read it through again, dissatisfied with the inadequacy of the words, the thoughts it contained. It didn't hold a fraction of the things she needed to tell him, but perhaps it said what he needed to hear.

Resolutely, she folded it, placed it in an envelope, and sealed it. She tried to tell herself not to expect too much, that her main reason for writing was simply to let him know she had been wrong. But Maggie knew she was lying to herself. Selfishly, she wanted the letter to make a difference, to bring a response from Mark that would show her that he returned her love even in some small measure.

She mailed the letter the next morning, then began an interminable period of waiting. She kept reminding herself not to get her hopes up, but she couldn't keep the warmth from welling up inside every time she thought of him.

Friday was the day she had decided the letter

would reach him, and when it came and went without a word, a feeling of defeat settled heavily on her spirit. After spending Saturday morning listlessly gazing out her window, she decided she would go to see Jake. She didn't even try to fool herself into believing she was going simply to talk with a sweet old man. She wanted to be near anyone who reminded her of Mark.

Two hours later she pulled into the gravel parking lot. She had called before she left, to make sure Mark would not be there, and had been surprised to find that Jake sounded anxious to see her. As she walked to the front door, she remembered the way he had taken her aside the day she had been here with Mark. Maybe Jake could give her a clue to Mark's feelings that would at least ease the questions in her mind so that she could settle down to a future without him.

The housekeeper showed Maggie into the living room, where Jake sat in front of a fire. The air was just beginning to hold a little nip, and the fire looked warming.

"Hello, darlin'," Jake said, rising stiffly. "I wondered when you were going to get around to paying me a visit."

"How are you feeling, Jake?" she asked, taking the hand he extended.

"I think old age is finally catching up with me," he said, chuckling softly, then settled back in his chair as Maggie sat on the sofa.

He looked at her suddenly, his pale eyes amazingly sharp. "What's going on between you and Mark, Maggie? He hasn't been to see me since he brought you, but when he phones his voice sounds tired. Tired and old." He raised an eyebrow, and Maggie caught her breath as his resemblance to

Mark struck her forcibly. "That boy has never been tired in his life. What happened?"

Maggie opened her mouth to heap the blame on her own head once more, then stopped suddenly. "I'm sick of telling myself how wrong and stupid I was, Jake," she said vehemently. "It wasn't *all* my fault. I know I was a coward, but, damn it, he didn't make it any easier. He deliberately played the fool and hid himself from me. If he had been more open, maybe I could have been, too, and we wouldn't be in this mess now." She leaned back against the sofa and closed her eyes. "What difference does it make anyway?" she asked wearily. "He's made it perfectly clear he doesn't want to see me. I wrote to him and apologized. I took all the blame on myself, and he ignored it."

"Maybe he's hurting too bad to see you right now," he suggested softly. "Are you sure he's already gotten the letter?"

"Yes, I'm sure. It's had more than enough time to get to him."

"I was afraid something like this would happen. I could see the way things were going when you were here before. That's why I wanted to talk to you. Mark wouldn't thank me for interfering, but I think there are some things you are entitled to know about him."

He paused as though to gather his thoughts, then began to speak slowly and quietly. "When Mark was staying with Jennie and me, he was the most open, loving boy you could ever hope to meet. He wasn't any angel, so don't get me wrong, but he was an outgoing, lovable, normal boy. Then, when he was fourteen, old Marcus took over. At first it didn't seem to make much difference, and I hoped that Mark would come through it all right.

Then"—he paused, closing his eyes briefly and clearing his throat before he continued—"then Jennie died. It was like his anchor was torn loose, and in my grieving I couldn't seem to help him. The open, loving boy got buried somewhere deep inside him, and a man I didn't know took over. Every now and then I'd catch a glimpse of the Mark I knew and I could see he was hurting, but there wasn't a damn thing I could do about it. He had closed himself off to everyone—me included." He sighed heavily. "I didn't have to ask him what was happening. I knew. I had been there before him. I know what superficial, money-worshiping people can do to person's soul, especially a man like Mark. When I was in that trap, I ran—as far and as fast as I could. Well, Mark did the same thing. He ran and hid—only, he did it in his head. He pretended that none of it bothered him. He saw the greed and those slobbering jackasses trying to lick his boots and he laughed. It was the only way he could find to fight it. He knew if he showed his grandfather and his so-called friends his true face, they would rip it to pieces. So he showed them a face they could accept."

"But me?" Maggie whispered, making no attempt to check the tears streaming down her face. "Couldn't he have been honest with me? Did he think I was like them?"

"Think about it, Maggie. This was not an overnight process. Think about how many years it took, how many times he got slapped in the face before he learned his lesson." He hesitated, then seemed to come to a decision, and continued. "I saw him looking at you the night you were here. He looked at you the way I used to look at Jennie. And I saw fear in his eyes, too. Maggie, yours is the one slap that would break him. I guess he just couldn't risk it. He learned his lesson too well."

"So what do I do now?" Her voice was tight from the hopelessness she felt. "I've told him I love him. What else can I do?"

"Just wait, Maggie. And don't give up on him. I have a lot of faith in him. He'll come through, all right."

I hope you're right, Maggie thought as she drove home. Oh, Lord, Jake, I hope you're right.

The rest of the weekend dragged, and by Monday morning as she dressed for work, Maggie decided that Mark had had long enough to make up his mind. It was time to take things into her own hands. What they had was too important to let slip through their fingers. She would dog his steps if she had to, as he had done with her. She would make him admit he loved her.

Please, she begged silently, let him love me. Then she shoved away the insidious doubts and picked up her purse on her way into the living room. She was walking toward the door to leave when the doorbell rang. Expecting a neighbor or Carrel, she opened the door—and found Mark standing there.

Momentarily paralyzed, she stood in silence. She couldn't have spoken if her life depended on it. His dear face was set in stern lines, but for a moment his expression made no impression. All that mattered was the fact that he was there. He had come, just as Jake had said he would. Maggie felt joy exploding in her mind, racing through her body, leaving her weak. He knew she loved him and he had come. That had to mean something.

Then, as he continued to stand there with that closed, hard look on his face, the doubts began to creep in again. The knowledge that she loved him evidently brought none of the joy to Mark that she was feeling. He made no move to touch her. He simply stood and stared.

"Mark," she began huskily. "I—"

"I want you to come with me, Maggie," he said, his voice stiff and unbending. "I have something I want to show you."

He took her arm, giving her no chance to accept or reject his stilted request, and spoke not one word to her until they had driven downtown and were in the elevator on their way to his office.

"Why did you bring me here?" she asked quietly.

"Because there are some things you need to know," he replied, his voice chilling. "I had hoped that this wouldn't be necessary, but apparently I was wrong. I went back to St. Thomas last week, and it gave me a chance to think. I finally decided that I would give you hard facts, since feelings don't seem to matter to you."

"You've been out of town?" she said in surprise. The possibility that he could be out of town had never occurred to her.

He looked at Maggie as though she were a little stupid. "Yes. I returned yesterday. Why?"

He hadn't received her letter. He couldn't have if he had only returned yesterday, for she had sent the letter to his office. So he didn't know.

"Mark," she said urgently, "I've got to tell you—"

"We can talk later, Maggie. I want you to have the facts first."

"But—"

"Later," he repeated sharply as he ushered her into his office.

John Lowe was seated in a chair beside Mark's desk. He rose as they entered, and shook Maggie's hand before Mark indicated that she should sit in the chair placed in front of his desk. He moved to sit in his own high-backed, swivel chair, then nodded to John.

"Miss Simms," he began after clearing his throat. "Mr. Wilding has asked me to bring you up to date on some of the activities he's been involved in over the past few years. I believe you'll find it a very impressive list." He smiled and glanced at Mark, who had turned his chair sideways as though uninterested in the proceedings, then cleared his throat again and continued. "When Mr. Wilding took over the company ten years ago it was still in the age of the dinosaur. It wasn't easy, because there were many who opposed him, but he brought it up to its present efficiency in just a few short years. What he did in simple terms was to . . ."

Maggie sat silently as Mr. Lowe began to lecture on the innovations Mark had made, not only in the parent company, but in all of the Wilding holdings. From there he went on to the labor reforms he had instituted, his work with charitable organizations, his activity as the prime mover behind the renovation of several historical sights around the state, and his periodic lectures at various Texas universities. She was bombarded by innumerable facts and figures for the next two hours. Then, smiling and nodding, John Lowe gathered his papers and left the room.

For several moments a heavy silence filled the office. Then Mark began to speak quietly. "Do you have any idea how demeaning it is for a man to have to convince someone he loves that he is worth her attention? After you politely suggested that I get lost, I told myself that if you couldn't love me without my having to prove myself, then I was better off without you." He turned to look at her, a strange, mocking smile appearing on his face. "But of course, that view didn't last long. After a hellish week without you I was brought forcibly to the conclusion that I would do whatever I had to do to get you. I can't say the realization made me ecstatic. It didn't. It made me feel weak and spineless. It's a very uncomfortable feeling, Maggie, and it's going to take me awhile to come to grips with it. Until then I think it would be best if you leave. Maybe later we can work something out, if you like, but not now." He closed his eyes and repeated, his voice strained, "Not now."

It took Maggie some time to absorb what he was saying. She had latched eagerly onto the fact that he had said he loved her, and the rest seeped in slowly through the cozy fog that enveloped her. He wanted her to leave. She had to tell him, make him understand that she loved him and had wanted him before Mr. Lowe's report.

"Mark, there is something that you should know."

"Please, Maggie, would you simply leave?" He leaned back in his chair. "I'm tired and I've got a half-dozen things to do before I can go home."

Maggie rose from her chair and walked to stand beside him. If she could touch him, she knew she could make him understand. "Listen to me, Mark. I sent . . ." She glanced down, and there, on top of a stack of mail, was her letter to him.

Mark's eyes followed hers, took in the letter, but showed no signs of comprehension. He stared at her for a moment, then rose abruptly to move away from her, saying, "Damn it, Maggie. What are you doing? If you have those blasted hiccups again, so help me, I'll strangle you." He moved to a wooden cabinet to pour himself a drink. "I have an appointment in five minutes, so we don't have time to discuss anything now."

She stared at him as he swallowed the drink in one gulp. Then she glanced back at the letter and shrugged. There was nothing she could do now. Eventually he would have to read the letter, and then he would know and understand. "Okay." She sighed. "If that's what you want." She turned and left the office.

What a holy mess, she thought as she took the elevator down to the lobby. She couldn't decide whether to laugh or cry. Every time it seemed as though things were going to work out between them, something else happened. It was all so crazy. She loved him and he loved her and they were still apart.

Mark loves me, she thought giddily, blocking out all the problems as the words formed again in her head, and they seemed so loud and clear that she looked around the elevator to see if anyone had noticed. But apparently no one had heard the joyous words, for they all seemed to be staring at the ceiling. She wanted to grab the world by the shoulders and shout, "He loves me."

As she walked down the street away from his office, Maggie smiled at strangers, perused the merchandise displayed in the windows—and took in absolutely nothing. Stopping before a small shop, she realized that it was familiar. This was the window that had held the brass unicorn. The unicorn had been dethroned by a red ceramic pig, and Maggie paused to stare at it, remembering. She had looked up that day and seen his reflection in the window.

Maggie looked up, and suddenly her reminiscent smile faded, her eyes widening in surprise. There, standing behind her, gasping for breath, was Mark. She whirled around to face him. "Mark!"

"Maggie, you little fiend," he said, breathing hard. "I'm too old to be chasing you down the street. Why in hell didn't you tell me about that letter?"

Before she could even formulate an answer he grasped her arm and began walking toward his office, pulling her along with him. She managed somehow to keep up with his long strides as he hurried her down the street and through the lobby to the elevator. She leaned gratefully against the elevator wall, trying to ignore the amusement of the other occupants.

When they reached the floor housing his office, she then had to face the curious stare of his secretary before finally reaching the solitude of his large office.

"Now," he said, closing the door behind her and leaning against it, "let's try to get this straight. You wrote that letter last week. Right?"

Maggie nodded silently.

"So my great martyr act was unnecessary?"

Maggie stifled a smile and nodded again.

"And you were trying to tell me about it when I very dramatically threw you out of my office?"

Maggie couldn't keep her lips from twitching as she nodded once more.

"And you're not going to make it one bit easier for me, are you? You're just going to stand there and let me make an even bigger ass of myself. Right?"

The smile could no longer be contained, and

she grinned openly as she said, "Right," then walked into his open arms.

"Oh, God, princess," he growled in her ear as he tried to meld her body into his own. "It's been so long. And I've been so hungry for you."

"I know," she whispered, burying her face in his chest, clutching him fiercely. "It's been awful."

"I thought I would go crazy," he murmured as he eased her down on the couch that lay along one wall of his office. "I would stay up until all hours of the night thinking of you. Then, when I would finally drift off to sleep, I would dream of you. And wake up to nothing."

"I'm sorry. I'm so sorry," she whispered urgently, touching his face, his throat, needing to confirm his presence. "It was my fault. I was so stupid."

"Hush," he said softly. "It doesn't matter now. All that matters is that you're here in my arms, where you belong." Pressing her back into the firm couch with his body, he buried his face in her throat, tasting the velvety skin with voracious kisses, smoothing the way with fingers that trembled. The buttons of her cream silk blouse were flimsy obstacles that fell quickly under his urgent siege. Then, without pause, he unclasped her lace bra, spreading the fabric of her blouse apart with hands that lingered on her swelling breasts. He watched with hungry eyes as her dusky rose nipples tautened and stood firm under his stroking thumbs.

Maggie caught her breath sharply as she felt his touch on her skin like tiny electric shocks. The pleasure sizzled through her flesh, and she moved convulsively as the tingling concentrated in her lower body. Without her volition, her hands reached up to draw his head down to her tumultuous breasts, and a groan, part pain, part pleasure, began in Mark's chest and was muffled against her rounded flesh.

He grasped her breast roughly with his hand as he nipped and stroked and sucked the erect tip avidly into his greedy mouth. He seemed to have lost all control, straining against her, pressing first one breast, then the other, into his heated mouth. He raised suddenly to jerk off his jacket and tie, then began to unbutton his shirt. Maggie reached up to help him but found her shaking fingers too uncoordinated to be of any use.

When the last button was freed, Mark leaned down slowly, his breath coming in short, raspy gasps. He was torturing her with his slow movements, and she felt she would shriek in frustration if she didn't feel his flesh against hers soon.

When the frustration had reached unbearable proportions, he reached down to slide his arm under her back and raised her the least fraction of an inch to meet him. She whimpered as the relief and pleasure—so incredibly acute—spread through her. She felt weak, as though her bones had been removed. Unable to move, she could merely lie there and feel.

But Mark suffered no such affliction. He moved against her urgently, each movement sending waves of sensation through her body. His hand slipped under her pleated skirt and slid down inside her panty hose, fondling her buttocks, squeezing them tightly before sliding around to clasp the heated, throbbing warmth between her legs.

Maggie cried out in unbelievable pleasure, writhing against his hair-roughened chest, his seeking fingers.

"God, princess," he whispered hoarsely. "I need

your magic now. I don't know if I can wait until we get home."

"I know, I know," she said softly through dry lips, her hand stroking his head soothingly as it lay on her breasts. "But someone could come in at any minute." She laughed shakily. "You certainly don't look like a dignified businessman right now."

"I don't feel like one, either," he said, turning his head to kiss her smooth, slightly tender flesh. "I've got a terrible problem, sweet."

"Oh?" she murmured, shivering in delight as she felt his lips touch the soreness of her breasts.

"Yes," he said. "I've got to figure out how to get us to your apartment without letting you out of my arms."

"That's a tough one, all right," she said, smiling in sympathy, then pressing his head closer. Although his voice sounded lazily casual, she could feel the frustration in his body. She wanted to soothe him, to bring him back from the high-pitched intensity of their interrupted lovemaking. She began to stoke his back, smoothing the taut muscles. But what began as aid to the man she loved soon turned into an exercise in tactile delight.

Her hands wandered over the warm, hard flesh, discovering every bone, every sinew in his strong back. She slid her palms down the ridge of his spine, over the sides of his trim waist, then back to slide her fingertips under his belt. Unable to stop the mesmerizing strokes, she moved her hand slowly around his side, then suddenly felt her fingers grasped and halted by his.

"Maggie," he said, his voice tight and hoarse. "I know you're trying to help, but if that's supposed to calm me, it's a total failure."

"Oh," she gasped, suddenly realizing what she

had been doing. "I'm sorry. I didn't mean . . . I was only trying to—"

"I know. And I appreciate your concern, but I don't think I can stand much more of your soothing without taking some definite and untimely action."

"Oh, Mark," she said, laughing at his rueful expression. "I've missed you so much. And it was all so dumb—I was so dumb."

"For heaven's sake, Maggie. Stop saying that." He raised up to look at her, then lay his head down again with a sigh. "You weren't any 'dumber' than I was. In fact, you showed remarkable intelligence compared to me. I knew what was happening. I could see so clearly where we were headed, but I couldn't—no, wouldn't—stop it. I didn't have the courage." He brushed his lips against her in an unconscious gesture, his eyes clouded with memories. "I was the clown, the court jester. I was afraid if I told you how desperately I loved you, you would laugh and make light of it, the way you did every time I hinted that I wanted more than an affair."

"But I thought you were joking," she protested, tightening her hold, feeling the hurt he must have felt at the time.

"I know, love," he soothed. "It wasn't your fault."

"Yes, it was," she insisted. "At least partly. I was all hung up on seeing you as a frivolous, superficial playboy, and I wouldn't let myself believe the evidence that was staring me in the face. And for the same reason as you: I was afraid. Afraid of failing again. What we had—have—was so beautiful, I couldn't take a chance on screwing it up." She laughed in disgust. "So I screwed it up."

"You didn't. You couldn't," he said softly. "I don't think anything could. Why do you think I pursued you the way I did? I knew that eventually, no matter what happened, we would be together. We had to be," he whispered, "or I would have lost myself, like in my dream."

"Your dream? The one you had in the cellar, then on St. Thomas?"

"That's the one." He shuddered and held her tighter. "The first time I had it was that night in the cellar." He grinned suddenly, his face looking years younger. "I was after you that night, love. From the first moment I saw you, I wanted you. And I'm not ashamed to say that I went to sleep that night with highly lustful thoughts filling my head. Then I had the dream. At first it didn't seem like a nightmare, merely a very strange dream. I was standing in a huge room—a ballroom perhaps—and I was surrounded by nebulous figures. Faceless people. Some male and some female, but all with a blank space where their faces should have been. At this point I began to feel a little uneasy. I began recognizing the figures as people I had known during my life. Don't ask me how. It wasn't as though I could see identifying marks or anything like that. I simply knew suddenly who they were. I remember seeing one of my closest friends, whom I had had dinner with only a few nights before. And standing next to him was the girl I was engaged to when I was twenty-four. The past and present were all jumbled together. And still I wasn't frightened. I simply knew that I didn't want to be there among all those faceless and, it seemed, soulless, people. Then I saw a huge gilded mirror hanging on one wall, the area around it deserted. I was drawn to it. I began to walk toward it even though I didn't want to. The closer I got, the stronger the feeling of dread became. I think I knew what I would see even before I stopped in front of the mirror, but that didn't make the shock, the horror, any less. When I looked into the mirror I saw that I was one of them. I was a nonperson, like everyone else in the room.

His voice was low and rough as he recalled the dream. Maggie shivered, stroking his face, sharing the terror with him as he took a deep breath and continued. "It was the most spine-chilling thing that had ever happened to me. You know how nightmares are. There's no logic, no reason, just overpowering terror. I was standing there facing the loss of my reality. Then I felt a peculiar sensation, as though the mirror had lost some of its power over me. I turned away and saw you." He hugged her closer, kissing her neck in a gesture of gratitude. "You were standing there in the middle of that ghoulish crowd, and reality seemed to shine out of you like dawn breaking on a dark night. In that moment it was as though I had X-ray vision, as though I could see clear to the heart of you, and I saw truth. You smiled at me, and the terror disappeared. You walked toward me then, and, Maggie"—he closed his eyes, remembering—"I seemed to swell and grow inside. When you stood beside me we turned together and looked again into the mirror. Somehow having you stand beside me had pulled me away from that false, nebulous world and I could see my own truth, my own reality, reflected in the mirror. As I stared at our images, I felt that I was on the verge of an important discovery. There was something I couldn't quite grasp, but I knew it was vital. Then you smiled again—a sad little smile—and began to walk away. The moment you left my side, my features began to blur and that debilitating terror returned. Then I woke up."

His voice faded and died, leaving an echo of the fear behind. Maggie had been so caught up in his nightmare, she felt weak with relief that it was finally over. "Lord, Mark," she breathed. "I can understand how it must have affected you. But if your love for me is based on that dream"—she paused and looked into his eyes—"I don't think I can live up to it. I'm not truth, justice, and the American way. I'm just me. Not all bad, but definitely not all good. Like I said in my letter, I'm totally fallible."

"Yes, I know, love," he said, chuckling as he raised himself on one elbow to kiss her. "That's what makes you so adorable." He kissed her again, slowly this time, then sat up, pulling her into his lap. "It took more than one dream to convince me. But still, I couldn't get it out of my mind after our night in the cellar. I also couldn't get your response to my lovemaking out of my mind," he added. "That's why I couldn't take no for an answer. Why I had to follow through. I had to know what the dream meant. I had to know if you held the key to my reality in your small hands."

"I guess I know what you mean," she murmured softly. "I had no dream, but during these past two weeks I've come to realize that you make me real. Only when I'm with you do I come to life."

"Oh, love," he sighed, laying his head back. "That's what I wanted but didn't dare hope for. When we were in St. Thomas it was so perfect. We came together as though we had been born specifically for the purpose of loving each other, and

I hoped—God, how I hoped—that you would love me back."

"You loved me then?" she asked incredulously.

He chuckled and gave her a bruising hug, his hand coming to rest on her bare breast. "I suspected I was in trouble the night I blew my chance to seduce you. Then in St. Thomas when you got those damned hiccups I knew I was lost. I wanted to hold you and protect you, even if it meant protecting you from myself. But of course"—he paused to kiss the tip of her nose—"you simply would not be protected and insisted on throwing yourself at me."

"I what?" she said indignantly. "I did no such thing, Marcus Wilding. You . . ." She stopped for a moment, then began to smile. "Come to think of it, I guess I did."

"Yes, you did," he said smugly. "For which I am eternally grateful. I was trying so hard to act honorably, but I'm afraid if you had held out much longer, honor would have gone right out the window."

"Ah, yes," she said. "My black knight. But you can't fool me any longer. You were the one who had Mr. Lowe read that interminable list of your virtues. So don't try to tell me you're a scoundrel."

"About that list, love," Mark said slowly, a grin beginning to spread across his features.

"Don't tell me you got that sweet little man to lie for you," she asked suspiciously.

"No . . . not exactly. It's just that those charitable things he told you about are forced on any man who is in my position. It's expected of me. So don't go thinking I'm your Sir Lancelot after all."

"Of course not," she said, smiling inwardly. It would take awhile before he trusted her enough to come out from behind his protective screen. Maggie wouldn't push it now. They had the rest of their lives. "I would never accuse you of being anything less than totally corrupt. But even if your armor is slightly tarnished, you happen to be the only knight I'll ever want."

"I'd better be," he said, framing her face roughly between his palms, then he repeated softly, "I'd better be." He lowered his head to kiss her lips, gently at first, then with a growing hunger. "Maggie," he murmured against her lips.

"Yes, darling?"

"Hadn't we better go home and get to work on curing those hiccups?"

She ran her hand over his chest, fascinated by the feel of him, then drew back to look at him as his words sank in. "But I don't have the hiccups."

He fastened her bra, then began to button her blouse before finally looking up to smile and say, "Don't you believe in preventive medicine?"

She stared at him and began to smile, then to laugh, and soon the sound of their laughter filled the room in a joyous premonition of the years to come.

Chapter Eleven

And the years that followed *were* filled with laughter, and some tears, and they overflowed with love. As Jake's health began to fail, Mark gradually broke away from his grandfather's empire. He and Maggie moved into the lodge, giving Jake the dubious pleasure of the presence of Marcus Wilding the Fifth.

Buster, as Jake dubbed the boy, was a scamp from the minute he was born. He had his mother's brown hair, his father's silver eyes, and a hard-headed personality all his own.

By the time Buster was born, Mark had stopped having the nightmare, but for the first year of their marriage he would periodically wake Maggie in the middle of the night as he writhed in the grip of the old horror. When he reached out for her in the darkness, she would soothe him in the only way she knew, with her body and her love.

One morning as Maggie turned back to the stove to finish cooking Buster's breakfast, she thought again of the relief she had felt when the dream finally let go of Mark. She'd known then that she had his complete trust.

She turned the bacon, then shoved two slices of bread in the toaster. And as she lifted her eyes from the toaster, she caught sight of Mark, standing outside the window, his face lifted toward the morning sun. And suddenly they were on the island again and she could see him standing naked and golden in the bright tropical sun. She felt the sensual touch of the sand beneath her feet, and her heart began to pound with desire.

He turned to see her watching him and walked closer to the window. But when he saw the hunger in her face and shining from her eyes, he switched his course and walked to the back door.

"Let's go back to the island," she said when he held her in his arms.

"The bedroom is much closer, love," he said against her throat. "Why don't we go back to the bedroom now and go to St. Thomas next week?"

"I didn't mean right this minute." She laughed. "But you do want to go back, don't you? I mean to our island. We've been to Charlotte Amalie to see Paul, but we haven't been back to that little turquoise cove."

"Yes, we'll go back," he whispered in her ear. "And we'll swim and we'll spread our blanket on the beach and . . ."

Before he could complete the intriguing sentence, they were interrupted by a small voice. "Mom! You're burning the bacon . . . again," the voice said in disgust.

"I'm sorry, Buster," she said, hurrying to remove the smoking skillet from the burner. "I'll make you some more."

"You'd better let me do it," he said in resignation. "When you and Dad start kissing, a person could starve to death. And besides, I'm almost as good a cook as you are."

"And modest, too," Mark said, pulling Maggie back into his arms.

Buster turned to look at them, and Maggie caught her breath as she saw her eight-year-old son's silver eyes sparkle with fun.

"Quite," he said casually, then turned to select another skillet.

Mark and Maggie looked at each other, stunned into silence for a moment; then they began to laugh under the indignant eyes of Marcus Wilding the Fifth.

THE EDITOR'S CORNER

The LOVESWEPT staff is small . . . but super . . . and I don't know what our authors or I would do without these three wonderful women. In LOVESWEPT tradition they'll introduce themselves to you in their own words.

"I'm Susann Koenig, Administrative Assistant to Carolyn. Although I'm fresh from college and new to publishing and the romance field, I feel I couldn't have found a better place to start! I've truly been caught up in the enthusiasm and excitement surrounding LOVESWEPT!"

"My name is Nita Taublib. I work three days a week on LOVESWEPT, primarily evaluating submissions. Carolyn and I started working together at Second Chance at Love about three years ago—and she still can't get rid of me. I decided to give her a second chance and followed her to Bantam where she just swept me away with responsibilities. She calls me the fastest reader in the East or West—but the truth is I'm just frugal. Why should I pay to read the best romances when I can read them for free?"

"My name is Elizabeth Barrett—and with a name like that, I simply had to work in romance! I started as an Editorial Assistant with Carolyn at Second Chance at Love, then moved to Silhouette Books as an Assistant Editor. I'm very happy to join Carolyn here at Bantam Books, and I'm delighted to be working on the LOVESWEPT line."

(continued)

Susann, Nita, and Elizabeth are just as thrilled as I to be able to help bring to you three more marvelous love stories next month.

Joan Domning does it again—creates for you a simply marvelous hero! In PFARR LAKE AFFAIR, #19, Eric Nordstrom has all the mischief and love of life of a boy, yet the magnetism and sensuality of a mature man. What a combination! And how could Joan's heroine, Leslie, possibly resist him? Well, for one thing, just imagine being wooed under the watchful eyes—and occasional applause—of a resort staff composed of college students! PFARR LAKE AFFAIR is a true delight, filled with touching humor.

Carla Negger's LOVESWEPT launch book, MATCHING WITS, got raves from readers and reviewers, especially for its humor. Well, she's back with an equally funny and utterly charming romance between the delightfully unconventional puppeteer, JoAnna Radcliff and the urbane, devastatingly attractive heart surgeon, Paul Welling. HEART ON A STRING, #20, shimmers with sensuality and originality and is sure to keep you riveted first page to last!

With just two published works, Fayrene Preston has established herself as a major romance writer. Following up her enormously popular LOVESWEPT launch book, SILVER MIRACLES, is another "miracle" of a book— THE SEDUCTION OF JASON! Never take "no" for an answer becomes the motto of heroine Morgan Sanders as she refuses to let Jason Falco give up the great love they share. And some of Morgan's tactics are outrageously clever. Wait until you read about Jason's reaction to Morgan renting a billboard. It proclaims her feelings and stands across from his corporate headquarters! THE SEDUCTION OF JASON is a deliciously different and very exciting love story you won't want to miss!

As always, we hope you truly enjoy each of these LOVESWEPT romances! Keep your cards and letters coming; we love hearing from you.

With warm good wishes,

Carolyn Nichols

Carolyn Nichols
LOVESWEPT
Bantam Books, Inc.
666 Fifth Avenue
New York, NY 10103

Love Stories you'll never forget by authors you'll always remember